Nate Williams has become one of the most powerful defense attorneys in Boston——I barely recognized him yesterday! He's polished and professional now, yet still seems haunted by his old sins. Little else seems to have changed about him, particularly his old crush on Kathryn Price. And poor Katie has had her own share of troubles lately——her career has stalled since her accident. She's been struggling far too long and deserves a chance at happiness.

Those two clearly have unfinished business with each other, but to build a future, Nate will have to face up to his deepest secrets. And Katie will have to stop living in the past, and see Nate for the man he has become. . . .

Dear Reader,

Well, as promised, the dog days of summer have set in, which means one last chance at the beach reading that's an integral part of this season (even if you do most of it on the subway, like I do!). We begin with *The Beauty Queen's Makeover* by Teresa Southwick, next up in our MOST LIKELY TO… miniseries. She was the girl "most likely to" way back when, and he was the awkward geek. Now they've all but switched places, and the fireworks are about to begin.…

In *From Here to Texas*, Stella Bagwell's next MEN OF THE WEST book, a Navajo man and the girl who walked out on him years ago have to decide if they believe in second chances. And speaking of second chances (or first ones, anyway), picture this: a teenaged girl obsessed with a gorgeous college boy writes down some of her impure thoughts in her diary, and buries said diary in the walls of an old house in town. Flash forward ten-ish years, and the boy, now a man, is back in town—and about to dismantle the old house, brick by brick. Can she find her diary before he does? Find out in Christine Flynn's finale to her GOING HOME miniseries, *Confessions of a Small-Town Girl*. In *Everything She's Ever Wanted* by Mary J. Forbes, a traumatized woman is finally convinced to come out of hiding, thanks to the one man she can trust. In Nicole Foster's *Sawyer's Special Delivery*, a man who's played knight-in-shining armor gets to do it again—to a woman (cum newborn baby) desperate for his help, even if she hates to admit it. And in *The Last Time I Saw Venice* by Vivienne Wallington, a couple traumatized by the loss of their child hopes that the beautiful city that brought them together can work its magic—one more time.

So have your fun. And next month it's time to get serious—about reading, that is.…

Enjoy!

Gail Chasan
Senior Editor

Please address questions and book requests to:
Silhouette Reader Service
U.S.: 3010 Walden Ave., P.O. Box 1325, Buffalo, NY 14269
Canadian: P.O. Box 609, Fort Erie, Ont. L2A 5X3

The Beauty Queen's Makeover

TERESA SOUTHWICK

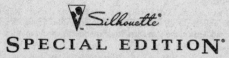

SPECIAL EDITION®

Published by Silhouette Books

America's Publisher of Contemporary Romance

Special thanks and acknowledgment are given to Teresa Southwick for her contribution to the MOST LIKELY TO... series.

 SILHOUETTE BOOKS

ISBN 0-373-24699-4

THE BEAUTY QUEEN'S MAKEOVER

Visit Silhouette Books at www.eHarlequin.com

Printed in U.S.A.

Books by Teresa Southwick

Silhouette Special Edition

The Summer House #1510
  "Courting Cassandra"
Midnight, Moonlight &
  Miracles #1517
It Takes Three #1631
The Beauty Queen's Makeover #1699

Silhouette Books

The Fortunes of Texas
Shotgun Vows

Silhouette Romance

Wedding Rings and
  Baby Things #1209
The Bachelor's Baby #1233
A Vow, a Ring, a Baby Swing #1349
The Way to a Cowboy's Heart #1383
And Then He Kissed Me #1405
With a Little T.L.C. #1421
The Acquired Bride #1474
Secret Ingredient: Love #1495
The Last Marchetti Bachelor #1513
**Crazy for Lovin' You* #1529
**This Kiss* #1541
**If You Don't Know by Now* #1560
**What If We Fall in Love?* #1572
Sky Full of Promise #1624

†*To Catch a Sheik* #1674
†*To Kiss a Sheik* #1686
†*To Wed a Sheik* #1696
††*Baby, Oh Baby* #1704
††*Flirting with the Boss* #1708
††*An Heiress on His Doorstep*
  #1712

*The Marchetti Family
**Destiny, Texas
†Desert Brides
††If Wishes Were...

TERESA SOUTHWICK

lives in Southern California with her hero husband who is more than happy to share with her the male point of view. An avid fan of romance novels, she is delighted to be living out her dream of writing for Silhouette Books.

~~To Katie, the coolest girl in school, and my~~
~~good friend.~~

~~To Kate~~

~~To Kath~~

Hey Katie,

You're a real cool girl and it's been awesome
hanging out with you.

Thanks for the fun times, and good luck with
your modeling. I bet you'll knock 'em dead.

Your ~~pal~~ friend,

Nate

Chapter One

All she'd wanted was to sit by the pool and feel the sun on her skin.

Today was the first day in a over a year that Kathryn Price had gone out in public without a scarf covering her face. She should have known better. Someone was coming and any second whoever it was would see what she'd been hiding.

If it would help, she'd shout "The British are coming," since she just happened to be staying at the Paul Revere Inn outside of Boston. But that would only attract the attention she was trying so hard to avoid. The voices on the other side of the hedge told her there was just enough time for a clean getaway. She wasn't ready to face people and when people got a good look at her face, the feeling was mutual. So she got up from the chaise lounge and headed for the other gate out of the pool area.

It had been a year since she'd been in the media spotlight. Three hundred and sixty-five days since her accident had been the lead story on the nightly news, not to mention magazines and tabloids. It was unlikely anyone would remember her as the model on her way to being the "it" girl. Now she was the poor unfortunate who would never make the swimsuit cover of *Sports Illustrated*—not with the scars left from repairing that shattered leg. The hardware holding it together would set off metal detectors at the airport. But on the off chance someone recognized her, she wasn't prepared to deal with curious stares and pitying glances.

As she hurried through the exit, she glanced over her shoulder, then slammed into what felt like a solid brick wall. The collision bounced her backward and she would have landed on her fanny except for the strong hands that reached out and grabbed her. But those same strong hands pinned her arms and she couldn't secure her oversize sunglasses, which had landed at her feet and left her bare face exposed.

"Whoa, Sparky." Laughter rumbled through his deep voice. "Where's the fire?"

Human contact. That was exactly what she'd been escaping from. And this was male human contact, her worst-case scenario. Damn it. Served her right for ignoring her gut feeling to stay in her room. She wasn't even sure what she was doing here. Well, that wasn't exactly true. Literally she was at this hotel because it was the only decent place to stay near Saunders University. And she was staying because her teacher, mentor and old friend from Saunders had sent out a distress signal.

"I'm sorry," she mumbled, stepping away from the stranger. "My glasses," she said, starting to pick them up.

"Allow me," he offered gallantly, then leaned over and beat her to it.

Once upon a time she'd been agile enough to make even this tall, athletic-looking man look like the tortoise to her hare. But the accident had changed that. And the fact that he was staring intently made her nervous. She half turned, keeping the left side of her face in shadow.

"May I have my glasses, please?" If there was a God in heaven, she sounded cool and controlled in a sophisticated sort of way. Not needy, insecure and wishing to be anywhere but here.

"Sorry. Of course. How could I refuse a pretty lady?"

Her? Pretty? Kathryn barely held back a bitter laugh. She used to be. But the accident had changed that, too. Nothing about her life was as it had been.

"Thank you," she said. "Now I'll be going and get out of your way."

She secured the glasses on her nose, and brushed her fingertips along her cheek to make sure everything was covered the way she wanted it. When she was satisfied, she glanced up and did a double take. The man could only be described as drop-dead gorgeous. In her line of work—make that former work—she'd met and posed with *People* magazine's sexiest man alive. This guy could win that cover hands down. He was the walking, talking, breathing embodiment of tall, tan, hunky heart-throb.

He was six feet two if he was an inch and his hair was shot with reddish-brown highlights. Brown eyes brimming with warmth and humor studied her from a face that was… Chiseled was a word straight out of a romance novel and probably a cliché. But she'd been out of circulation too long to be up on the current catchy slang and her brain was shouting hubba hubba so loud, she couldn't think of a better description. So, chiseled worked for her.

His nose was perfectly straight, his jaw square with a hint of an indentation. It was a lean, handsome face—and his body was a perfect match. She knew quality when she saw it and the expensive navy-blue suit was tailor-made, setting off his wide shoulders to perfection. The red power tie was the cherry on top of a very impressive sundae. For a lot of reasons, she wasn't easily impressed. But he was flawless. It was a lot of information to pick up in a glance, so it must have been the double take. Although it was useless information. She'd never been very good with men and she didn't need more information to process the fact that this one was way out of her league.

"I have to go now," she said.

He didn't move aside. "Don't tell me. Let me guess. You're the White Rabbit? And you're late for a very important date?"

Her? A date? Hardly. If only she *could* be the Rabbit and escape down the rabbit hole. But escape seemed less urgent somehow. There was something about his voice—a sensation of comfort as the warm richness of it drizzled over her like melted fudge. A memory nipped at the edge of her mind but refused to crystallize. For some weird reason and against all the odds, the urge to flee from this stranger faded.

Finally, she moved from dappled shade into sunlight and looked directly into his eyes. The friendly expression instantly turned to astonishment. "Katie?"

That stunned her. No one had called her that since college. Who was he? And what did he know about her? The mirror had become her worst enemy, but she wished for one now. She'd made very sure the glasses covered everything. Unlike Mr. Perfect, she had a lot to hide.

She studied him intently. "Do I know you?"

He mumbled something that sounded like, "Why should you? No one else does."

"What?"

"Nothing." He smiled. "More important—*I* know *you*. You went to Saunders University. As it happens, I was lucky enough to be there at the same time."

"Really?"

"I doubt you'd remember me."

Surely he was wrong. There were things she didn't want to remember, but someone so good-looking would be hard to forget.

"What's your name?" she asked.

His gaze slid away almost shyly, but his bearing and confidence didn't peg him as a shy man. "Nate Williams," he finally said.

Then he tensed slightly, as if bracing for a reaction. She probably only noticed because it was a habit she'd adopted—waiting for the shock, then the discomfort when a stranger's glance skittered away. But his name didn't jog her memory.

She shook her head. "Did we take a class together?"

"I was two years ahead of you and in prelaw."

"Then probably that's not how we met. I was never that focused." She tapped her lip as she thought back to the days that should have been carefree and were anything but. "What kind of activities were you involved in? Maybe we shared the same interest and that's where our paths crossed."

He shrugged. "I didn't have a lot of interests or extra time."

Which told her precisely nothing, and didn't help at all in placing him. She shook her head. "I'm sorry. I don't remember you."

He smiled. "Don't worry about it. That was a long time ago. It's no big deal."

"But you remember me."

"How could anyone forget? You were a big deal. The prettiest girl on campus. Voted most likely to wind up a cover girl. And you did. Of course I remember you."

Oh, God. He knew she'd been a model. Did he know anything else? "I really have to go."

"Not yet. Please?"

Good humor radiated from him and his eyes sparkled with a sincere something she hadn't seen in a man's expression for longer than she could remember. So long, in fact, she was surprised she'd recognized the blatant male appreciation. How was it possible to feel so warm and wary at the same time?

"Stay just a little longer. It's not often a guy like me gets to be this close to the face that launched a thousand lipsticks. And eye shadows, too, if I'm not mistaken."

Before she could stop him he removed her sunglasses and she gasped. There was no hiding now; he was up close and personal with her face. In front of God and everyone her scars were out there—the half circle groove over her left cheekbone, cut by her glasses in the same accident that shattered her left leg. Maybe now that he could see she was no longer the prettiest girl on campus he would move his larger than life self out of her way and let her go. She braced for his recoil of surprise followed by the poor-Kathryn-Price look.

She saw neither. His pleasant expression never changed. No, she thought, looking closer. It changed slightly with what might have been understanding flickering in his eyes. In spite of that, tension coiled in her belly. After he'd gone overboard about her model's face, she didn't dare hope that he would ignore the way she looked now. She wondered if he'd been living under a rock that he hadn't heard what had happened. He'd want to know the details and offer condolences. Finally he'd insist it was hardly noticeable, which she knew was a big fat lie. She'd only lost partial vision in one eye. She wasn't blind.

She braced herself again. Okay, she thought, let's get it over with. Then she could make good on this disastrous escape attempt and retreat to the privacy of her room, which was where she should have stayed in the first place.

She lifted her chin, met his gaze and held out her hand, palm up. Dignity was something the accident hadn't taken from her. "May I have my sunglasses back?" she asked, forcing a pleasant tone into her voice.

One corner of his mouth curved up. "Didn't anyone ever tell you guys dig chicks with scars?"

Of all the things he could have said, that was the most unexpected. She blinked at him, then felt a rusty, reluctant smile curl her lips. "No, but I've heard chicks dig guys with scars."

Directness was something she hadn't prepared for; it completely disarmed her. His quirky question, not ducking the obvious put her completely at ease. And she would never have believed it possible from a guy who looked as if he could be on the cover of *GQ* or *FITNESS FOR FANATICS*. How did he know just the right thing to say?

"It's true," he insisted. "A tangible sign of character. Guys always look for character."

"Oh, please. You're telling me character is the first thing you look for in a woman and not the size of her—" She held her hands out chest high and slid him a wry look.

He grinned. "In all those articles about the top ten things that attract one person to another, isn't sense of humor at the top of the list?"

"None of my friends store their sense of humor here, yet it's often where male eye contact starts. And what makes a person laugh is very different from character. I should know. I've been on the cover of magazines where those articles appeared. It seems to me looks top the lists."

"Then, clearly the articles are wrong."

"I appreciate that you're trying to make me feel better."

"Is it working?" he asked, hopefully.

"It would if I had my sunglasses."

He looked down at the glasses in his hand as if he'd forgotten he'd taken them off and still had them. He met her gaze and sighed dramatically.

"Okay, you can have them back. But only because it's sunny and squinting will give you crow's-feet around those beautiful eyes. Certainly not because the prettiest girl on campus has anything to hide."

"You are so lying," she said, shaking her head with a tentative smile.

A sudden frown chased the humor from his eyes and he looked almost nervous as he ran his fingers through his short, thick hair.

She put her hand on his arm. "You look like someone made a kite tail out of your favorite tie. That was a joke. Where's *your* sense of humor?"

"Joke. Right. I knew that."

Nate breathed a sigh of relief when she showed no signs of recognition. Although she was right about him lying—a lie of omission. But a lie by any other name was still a lie. He'd only told her his name, not who he really was. He'd never expected to see her again, not in the flesh. Pictures of her in magazines had been his only contact since college and all he could ever hope for. But a little over a year ago he'd lost track of her. Obviously something traumatic had happened to take her out of circulation.

She put her sunglasses back on. "I'm surprised you didn't ask how it happened."

He knew "it" was some kind of accident. "Do you want to tell me?"

"No."

The response was succinct, decisive and unequivocal. He slid his hands into the pockets of his slacks. "That's good enough for me."

If anyone could understand not wanting to discuss scars, it was Nate. And not all of them had been on his face. Severe teenage acne had left his face badly marked. As if that wasn't enough to deal with, his nose was broken in a college fight. Those were the days when everyone made fun of his "crater face." Everyone but Katie. She'd hung out at his fraternity house with her boyfriend. The jerk never passed up an opportunity to pick on the brainer geek who desperately tried to avoid him and fade into the woodwork.

Every time Nate was the butt of another joke, Katie made it a point to find something nice to say to him, and her sweetness managed to neutralize the filth from whatever dirt was shoveled his way. He would always be grateful to her for that. He wasn't lying about her character. To him, her heart and soul had always been even more beautiful than her face. And that was saying something because he also hadn't been lying about her being the prettiest girl on campus. She'd always wanted to be a model. He wondered about the state of her career now.

In college, the few who were acquainted with Nate Williams knew him as Wide Load Willie or Zit-face Willie. At the time, the nicknames were humiliating and he'd never expected to be grateful for them. But he was now. Because Katie didn't know him by his given name. When he'd finally joined a top legal defense firm and started making some money, he'd gone to a plastic surgeon who specialized in scar removal, had his nose fixed and hired a personal trainer to get him in shape. There was nothing left of Wide Load Willie and he no longer faded into the woodwork. Improved appearance had given him the confidence to take center stage in his career.

But when he'd introduced himself a few moments ago, there was no sign of recognition. Thank God. He didn't want her to remember the flabby-freak-with-no-friends he'd been. Today, when she'd finally looked at him, she liked what she saw. Since he'd never expected to see an expression of admiration in Katie Price's eyes, he liked that she liked him. And he didn't care if he was acting like a hormone-riddled high schooler.

He'd come a long way since college. He was a criminal defense attorney now, and his services were available to whoever could pay his price. But he didn't want to share that with her, either. It had given him the means to fix what was wrong with him on the outside, but lately he'd begun to wonder if the profession wasn't creating new, worse flaws on the inside. Many of his clients had little or no decency, honesty, integrity or morality. His grandmother used to say people are a product of their environment. What did that make him?

Katie snapped her fingers. "Earth to Nate? You drifted off. Stay with me here."

He shook his head, scattering the disturbing images—past and present. "Sorry. I have a bad habit of getting lost in my own thoughts. It's trademark brainer geek. You may remember."

Although he prayed she wouldn't.

She tapped her lip. "I can't picture you that way. In fact, I'm getting nothing from my memory banks."

His banks were overflowing with recollections. And the woman before him still had the same thick, silky dark brown hair. She was small for a model; the top of her head came about to his shoulder. Always thin, the sleeveless blouse and ankle-length skirt she wore made her look more fragile than he remembered. And when she shifted her weight from her left leg to her right, he didn't miss the wince—or the way she pressed a hand to the small of her back as if she was uncomfortable. He frowned. She didn't want to talk about it. But he was interested in everything about her, including what had taken the sparkle from hazel eyes he remembered flashing with energy and life.

He might be having a crisis of conscience about being a defense attorney, but he was damn good at it. And he didn't get where he was by refusing to ask the tough questions. He would find out about her—what she had done in the last ten years, and what she was doing now. But he would sit her down for the cross-examination.

He pointed down the path. "There's a cozy little bench just around the bend. It could take a while for us to catch up and you'd be doing an old man a favor if you'd sit down with me."

She hesitated a moment as she studied him. Finally she nodded and a small smile turned up the corners of her full lips as she said, "Old my eye."

He released a long breath and realized how much he hadn't wanted her to say no.

They walked slowly along the picturesque, landscaped cobblestone path. Manicured bushes and pink, purple and yellow flowers lined the way and swayed in the afternoon breeze. Stately old trees shaded them when they were settled on the bench, and he casually rested his arm along the back, his fingers just an inch from her shoulder.

"So you're a lawyer?" she asked, shifting slightly away from him.

The question drew his gaze to hers. Did she remember something about him? Maybe something she'd seen on the news? But her look was curious, if a little guarded.

"What makes you think that?"

"It was the prelaw information that gave me a clue."

"Oh," he said sheepishly. He wasn't normally such a dimwit. The power surge from being this close to her must be frying his brain. "Right. Yes. I'm a defense attorney."

"Must be nice to set a goal and reach it," she said wistfully.

"I suppose."

He'd always wanted to go into law, although he hadn't exactly followed the path he'd intended. But it wasn't himself he wanted to talk about. The breeze stirred the leaves overhead and he watched the dappled shadows dance over the lovely curve of her cheek and jaw. The scarred side of her face was in shadow, but it didn't matter. She was still the most beautiful woman he'd ever seen.

"Is your husband here with you?" he asked, fishing for information and hoping it didn't look like it. He hadn't felt this awkward around a woman in a very long time.

"That would be tough to pull off," she said.

"Why's that?"

"I'm not married." She tilted her head to the side as she studied him. "What about you?"

"I'm not here with anyone, either."

"You know that's not what I meant."

"I'd like to think personal interest made you nosy about my marital status."

She shook her head. "You're impossible."

"So I've been told. And for the record, I'm not married."

For just a second, she looked pleased, then her mask of cool unconcern was back. His fingers itched just to touch her, to make sure he wasn't dreaming and she was really there. But he sensed some tension in her and put his self-control firmly in place.

"So, how does it feel being back at Saunders?" he asked.

She glanced around. "The town hasn't changed much. Unlike Los Angeles, there are no palm trees. It's all a little run-down, just the way I remember. Although I'm sure the university Web site only highlights the green rolling hills and tree-covered campus with lots of stately buildings."

He laughed and nodded. "You nailed it, lady."

"How about that? Being a lawyer, you're the one who should have a way with words."

If she only knew, he thought. "So you're a model."

"Was." Absently she traced her cheek beneath the rim of the sunglasses covering half her face.

"Did you like it?"

She linked her fingers in her lap and he could almost see her knuckles turn white. "Yes. I was lucky. A girl like me with no particular skills would have difficulty making a good living otherwise."

"Who says you have no skills?"

"Oh, you know. Judging people on the outside. 'If she looks like that, she can't possibly have a single intelligent thought.'"

"That's ridiculous. I certainly never felt that way."

"Then you were in the minority. And it's not an issue any longer," she said with a huge sigh.

In his job he learned to read body language—witnesses, defendants and juries. The way her mouth pulled into a straight line told him she didn't want to say more. And if he pushed, she was outta there. So he decided to change the subject.

"What brings you back here?"

"Do you remember Professor Gilbert Harrison?" she asked.

"Do I? He was my favorite teacher."

She nodded. "Mine, too. He sent me a message that he's having some sort of trouble with the college Board of Directors and needed my help."

"I got the same message. And I've been nosing around."

"Do you know what's going on?" she asked.

He shook his head. "But where there's smoke, there's usually fire. And that's what worries me. I can't imagine the administrative body of a well-respected university going on a witch hunt without just cause."

"But what reason could there be? He was always popular. A lot of my friends took his classes and used to hang out at his office. Do you remember how crowded it always was?"

Nate didn't because he'd never seen the professor during his regular office hours. He'd had to hold down a job and take care of his grandmother. The professor had made time for him whenever he needed it.

"He's a good teacher and was a generous friend to me," he said, not quite answering her question, a defense lawyer tactic. "I'll always be grateful to him for his help."

Without it, he might not have made it through college—in spite of his high IQ. It was the stepping stone to law school and now he was considered one of the top defense attorneys in the country. Some of his defendants were notorious, which gave him more than his share of publicity. Katie didn't remember him from college, and she'd given no clue she knew who he was now. But the way she'd tried to hide from him when they ran into each other was a big sign she wouldn't relish any spotlight, even if it was collateral damage from him.

"He always did his best to help. That's the way I remember him, too," she said. "I wonder what's going on."

"Not a clue," he admitted.

As they talked, he could see her relaxing with him and he wanted to keep it that way. His gut told him if she knew the finer points of his identity and profession, she'd run far and fast. And he very much didn't want her to run. She'd been the single bright spot in his college experience. She'd been the reason he got out of bed every day—that and a dirt-poor kid's obsession to get an education and make money. But now that he'd found her again, he intended to be *her* bright spot.

"I've been thinking."

"Uh-oh, there's a dangerous prospect. I thought I just saw the lights flicker with the power drain."

"Very funny." She was definitely relaxing. "As I said, I've been nosing around here at Saunders."

"Why?"

"Just trying to gather information. Thought it might be helpful."

"And is it?"

He shrugged. "It might be if I had any. I'm getting nowhere. Either I can't get in to see anyone or the people I talk to claim to know nothing about anything."

"And?"

"It's time for me to go see Professor Harrison."

"And?" she said again.

"I was wondering if you'd consider going with me."

Nate held his breath while she thought over his suggestion.

"I'd like that," she finally said.

He'd like that, too. More than she knew. More than he wanted her to know. Because he very much wanted time with her. Time to replace the shadows in her eyes with the sparkle he remembered.

But he knew that if she remembered him, time wouldn't be his friend.

Chapter Two

"Hello, Professor Harrison."

Kathryn stood just inside the office doorway and felt Nate's warm hand on the small of her back. With an effort she controlled a shudder. The contact was supportive—a gentlemanly gesture, in no way threatening. But ever since that terrible night in college, she couldn't trust even the most innocent touch of a man. Ted Hawkins had stolen that from her.

Then she felt the professor's gaze on her and tensed for his reaction to her altered appearance. She realized her mentor had changed, too. His dark hair was graying now and his face was thinner, the lines beside his nose and mouth were craggy, as if carved and weathered. If his formerly warm, sparkling brown eyes were the window to his soul, it was fading fast. He stared, almost as if he didn't see them.

The man she remembered would have stood and greeted them affably—and been delighted that her vocabulary included that word. She'd deliberately not worn her sunglasses, to get through the awkwardness as quickly as possible. The man she knew would have observed the scars on her face and known just the right thing to say. That man was gone.

His white, long-sleeved shirt was rumpled, the trademark bow tie askew. Absentminded professor was a cliché, but he certainly looked the part. More troubling was the fact she'd never known him to be forgetful, distracted or inattentive. He'd always been sharp and insightful, with a wealth of obscure information at his fingertips. Whatever had compelled him to ask for help must be serious—something was taking a terrible toll on this man.

Then she realized he was studying Nate. She glanced at him and saw tension in the line of his broad shoulders, the muscle contracting in his lean cheek.

He moved in front of the desk and held out his hand. "Nate Williams, Professor."

"I know who you are," the older man said a little impatiently. Then he looked at her and smiled. "Kathryn Price." As if he finally remembered his manners, he held out his hand indicating the two chairs in front of his desk. "It was good of you to come. Please, sit down."

"Thank you." Kathryn sat.

Nate remained standing and gripped the back of the chair beside hers. When he spoke, the warm, melted-chocolate tone was missing from his voice. "What's going on, Professor? Why did you send for us?"

Nate had morphed from the good-natured, self-confident hunk who'd single-handedly brought her sense of humor back to life into an ultraserious man who tweaked something in her memory. But, again, whatever it was wouldn't shape up. She'd thought this setting would be familiar and possibly trigger memories of him. She'd been wrong.

At least some things didn't change. This office—a gazillion books filling the shelves, scattered papers on the desk, photographs on the walls—was just as she remembered.

"What's going on?" the older man repeated, glancing first at Nate, then her. "My job is in jeopardy."

"No. That's impossible."

"Unfortunately, my dear, it's all too possible."

Kathryn leaned forward. "But why? You've been at Saunders for years. What about tenure?"

"Tenure can't protect any educator against charges of impropriety. The Board of Directors is investigating me, looking for anything they can find and make stick."

"Why would they do that?" she asked.

"Rumors. Innuendo. Maybe a little jealousy of my rapport with students." He waved his hand dismissively.

"Will they find any evidence of impropriety?" Nate asked, his tone more gentle.

"Of course they won't." Kathryn frowned at him. He'd said where there's smoke, there's fire. If Nate believed the professor was guilty, why would he have come back to help? "I can't believe you asked him that."

"He's right to ask," the professor said.

"It's a defense attorney thing. Some don't want to know." Nate briefly met her gaze as he leaned his forearms on the chair back. "Others do so they don't put a client on the witness stand and risk perjury or self-incrimination. I prefer to know the good, bad and ugly up front because I don't like surprises."

The professor glanced away as he said, "They're looking for a way to get rid of me. I think some of it is about my age."

Kathryn met Nate's gaze. "Age discrimination is illegal, though, isn't it?"

"Yes," he confirmed.

For the first time since she saw him, Professor Harrison smiled. "Smart girl."

"Thank you." Kathryn glowed at the compliment. Not everyone had looked past her face to give her IQ the benefit of the doubt. From now on, she thought, brains were going to have to be enough.

The professor leaned forward and rested his elbows on his desk. "No one has come right out and said anything directly about my age. They're saying I'm unprofessional. Can't be such a 'pal' to the students. Can't hold their hand. They're in college now. Teachers have to keep a certain distance. Liability issues and such."

"They're wrong." Kathryn's heart went out to him. "It's a style thing. If I remember right, your approach was that you catch more flies with honey than vinegar. Many students owe you a lot."

"I'm one of them," Nate said. "I wouldn't be where I am today if not for you."

"So you're happy with the way things turned out?" the professor asked.

"Of course," Nate said automatically. "But I still don't understand why you sent for us."

The professor sighed as his faded brown eyes regarded them gravely. "I was hoping some of my former students would come back and put in a good word for me."

"We'd be happy to," Kathryn said, glancing up at Nate, who nodded agreement. "But how will that help?"

"A good question. Especially with Sandra Westport stirring up a hornet's nest."

"Sir?" Nate said, clearly puzzled. It was one single, respectful form of address to get the older man back on track.

"I'm sorry. That's another story. I was hoping you could simply tell the board that my method of teaching made a difference. That the career path you've chosen is of benefit to mankind and might not have happened but for my guidance and educational support."

"You want us to make them believe you have wings, a halo and walk on water?" Nate said wryly.

A smile pulled at the corners of the professor's mouth. "Is that so very far from the truth?"

"Just a little," Nate said, holding up his thumb and forefinger close together.

"I wouldn't dream of putting words in your mouth. But, I do hope I've been of some help in setting you

on your paths. One likes to think it made a difference."
He looked sad, suddenly, and miserable. "I've dedicated my life to teaching. Being around young people has always been very important to me and it's all I have now."

"That can't be true," Kathryn protested.

"But, it is, you see. My wife died not long ago. And I haven't always been…" He had a faraway look in his eyes as he sighed. "I feel as if I've lost so much. I don't think I could bear it if my job—my career were taken away, as well. There's so much more good I can do. I'm hoping that they'll see what I've accomplished and show leniency and compassion."

Nate frowned. "No one knows words like an English professor," he commented. "You're the best teacher I ever had. I swear you made me memorize the *Ninth Collegiate Dictionary* from cover to cover."

Another fleeting grin from the old man. "You're exaggerating, my boy."

"Only a little. But I know firsthand your intricate understanding of words and knack for choosing just the right one. You were forever after me to put a finer point on whatever I was trying to convey."

"And what is it you're trying to convey now, Nate?"

"That leniency is an odd choice of words for a man who's above suspicion."

"You always were too bright for your own good," the professor mumbled.

"What do you mean?" Kathryn asked, his words giving her a bad feeling.

He shook his head. "Just that no one is perfect.

Everyone has regrets, things they wish it were possible to go back and change."

Kathryn knew he was right. If she had it to do over, she'd never have dated Ted Hawkins in college. Professor Gilbert had tried to warn her, but she hadn't listened. Then it was too late. The thought made her shiver, making her angry with herself. She tried so hard to bury all this. Yet here she was acting as if it had happened yesterday.

"Hindsight is twenty-twenty," Nate commented, echoing her thoughts. "And regrets are not an actionable offense."

"He's right," Kathryn agreed, shaking off her own demons.

"I like being right." He grinned down at her, then it faded. When his glance went to the older man, he shifted nervously. "But without knowing specifics of the allegations, I'm not sure what I can say in your defense."

"Unfortunately, I can't be more specific," the professor protested. He looked down at his hands, folded on his desk. "It's all very complicated. But there's someone involved—a…a benefactor who wishes to remain anonymous."

"Like the Lone Ranger?" Nate asked.

"Hardly that heroic," the professor said. "No mask. No silver bullets or white stallions. This person simply helped students. Made it possible for some to receive an education who might not otherwise have been able to attend college. That sort of thing."

"And he doesn't want to be thanked?" Kathryn asked.

"I never said it was a 'he.'" The professor's tone was sharp. "I'm sorry. I simply cannot say anything else. I won't break a confidence." His eyes narrowed as he looked at Nate. "And I understand you've become very adept at getting people to let unintended information slip."

"It's my job to ask questions," Nate said, the words clipped. "That's what attorneys do."

"And isn't it lucky for the professor that you are one," Kathryn said, wondering what was going on between the two men. "He might need legal counsel if this goes any further."

"If Sandra Westport has her way it will go very far."

"You mentioned her before," Kathryn commented. "What is she doing?"

"Her husband, David, was one of my students. They met here at Saunders and fell in love. Now they own a store in Boston and she's a journalist for her small, hometown newspaper. Unfortunately her nose for news has her sniffing my way." The professor sighed. "She's inordinately curious about what she calls 'the mysterious patron.' This is a very sensitive time for me. While my job is in jeopardy, it would be better if she ceased her inquiries. The uproar she's creating is channeling suspicion toward me. Not that she'll find anything," he hastily added.

"Maybe Nate could help," Kathryn suggested. The words popped out before a cohesive thought had formed in her mind. But the idea had merit. He was an attorney. It was his job to sway opinion. "Maybe he could talk to Sandra Westport and convince her to drop her investigation."

Nate met her gaze, then nodded at the professor. "Of course. Whatever I can do."

Kathryn sighed. "You're a wonderful role model and mentor, Professor Harrison. You're the first person who challenged me. The first who made me consider the possibility that I'm more than just..." She stopped and looked down.

"A pretty face?" the professor said gently.

She met his gaze. For the first time since entering his office she saw the kindness and compassion in his expression that she remembered from all those years ago.

"Yes," she admitted. Absently, she touched her fingertips to the groove on her cheek. "Boy, that sounds conceited and so stuck-up. And ironic."

"I never knew you to be vain," the older man said kindly. "The young woman I knew was honest and self-aware and to the best of my knowledge never said an unkind word to anyone."

"Th—there was an accident—" Her voice caught and she stopped. "My face—isn't the same."

"No. Neither is mine." He glanced up. "For that matter, neither is Nate's."

"Some of us are just late bloomers," Nate said, an edge to his voice as a muscle in his cheek jumped.

"The point is," the professor said, meeting her gaze again, "appearance is not a person's defining essence. It's simply one part of the whole, which is constantly changing."

She smiled ruefully. "You're just giving me philosophical spin."

He shrugged. "Philosophy is attitude, and that can make all the difference. For what that's worth."

"It's worth a lot. Unlike anything I might have to say to the board on your behalf."

"You've always underestimated yourself, my dear."

She shook her head. "You sent out a call for help to your former students who made something of themselves. But I have to ask—why me?"

"How can you say that?" Nate protested.

She glanced up at the man still standing beside her. "You said it yourself—this is the face that launched a thousand lipsticks. That's not a cure for cancer or a plan for world peace. It's superficial and unimportant."

"Not to the cosmetics industry," Nate commented.

"How very defense attorney of you," she said wryly. "But the fact is I don't know if I can help. I'm not sure that anything I say will carry any weight. I'm not noble. I've done nothing very important with my career, or my life. For that matter, I don't even have a life. I don't know who I am anymore."

The professor smiled. "Then I would say your return to Saunders University is fortuitous."

"How do you mean?" she asked.

"At the risk of a clichéd metaphor, roots are the best place to dig for bits of yourself. Your roots are here at college. Unless I miss my guess, this is where you truly began to blossom."

Nodding absently, she thought about what he said. "Maybe. But I wish it wasn't your misfortune that brought me back."

"Every cloud has a silver lining." When the professor laughed, he sounded out of practice. "I seem to be in rare form today—clichés everywhere."

Kathryn stood. "Don't worry, Professor. Nate and I will do everything we can to help you."

* * *

And helping the professor was the blind leading the blind, Nate thought. He pulled his BMW into a space in the hotel parking lot and turned off the ignition, then went around to the passenger side to open Katie's door. It was a miracle she was still there—a miracle the professor hadn't let the proverbial cat out of the bag. If he hadn't been so preoccupied with his own troubles, he could easily have expanded on Nate's talent for eliciting information. Or how much he'd changed since college. Fortunately, he'd done neither.

"Here we are," he said, after he'd opened her door and held out his hand.

She looked at it for several moments before tentatively accepting. "Thank you."

"Although I'm not exactly sure where 'here' is," he admitted. "And I don't mean that literally."

"I knew that. The professor wasn't much help," she said, falling into step beside him.

"If anything, he created more questions than he answered," he said ruefully.

"At least we know what the problem is and what we can do to help."

"Yes."

To give the college board of directors a testimonial on how the professor influenced him on a career path to benefit humanity. Nate supposed a defense attorney fell into that category, although some compared him to a shark. He had the reputation of being less concerned about the merits of a case than a defendant's ability to pay for his billable hours. He also had a reputation for winning.

His services were sought after and he was in a position to pick and choose his clients. He picked the ones who could afford him. Long ago he'd realized knowledge was power and knowledge of the law was the power to make a difference for the less fortunate. Like his grandmother. Lately he'd had a nagging feeling the woman who'd raised him after his parents died wouldn't approve of the man he'd become. And now he wasn't so sure the slick lawyer he'd become could convince anyone that what he did was a help to humanity. But he'd try. For the professor.

"So what do we do now?" Katie asked.

Their footsteps clicked on the lobby's marble floor as they walked to the elevator. He pushed the up button. "We need to arrange to give our testimonials to the board. Earlier today I tried to see the administrator, Alex Broadstreet."

"And?" She looked up at him expectantly.

He shook his head. "He blew me off. Technically his secretary did, but he's calling the shots."

"Judging by the expression on your face, you're not a happy camper."

"Let me count the ways," he said grimly. "I was hoping this was all a misunderstanding and could be resolved with a simple conversation."

"Of course now we know that's not going to happen."

"No. In fact when I bumped into you earlier—"

"Literally."

He smiled. It was the best collision he'd had in a long time. The elevator arrived and they stepped inside. "Yes. I'd just come from trying to see Broadstreet."

"Is there a problem? Other than the obvious, I mean."

"I live two hours away. On the other side of Boston. I'd planned to resolve this and drive home tonight."

"Pride goeth before a fall," she said.

She didn't know how right she was. He wasn't used to failing. But a recent case and now this were giving him lessons in humility. Still, seeing her again made him wonder if this fall wasn't a blessing in disguise.

"Is that a nice way of saying I'm arrogant?" he teased.

"If the shoe fits…" She shrugged. "Are you?"

"Let's just say I wouldn't have to use the shoehorn on that one. Or I could plead the fifth—don't want to incriminate myself."

"So you didn't meet your objective today. Couldn't you call for an appointment and come back?" she suggested.

"I could. But my gut tells me that he's going to dodge phone calls. I think being on site and in his face is the only way I'm going to get anywhere."

"You may be right. This whole thing is weird and seems awfully cloak-and-dagger."

"It does feel as if they're trying to keep it quiet and railroad the professor without due process."

"I did promise we'd do everything we can to help him," she said. "And you promised you'd try to get Sandra Westport to drop her investigation," she reminded him. She shook her head. "But two hours is a long drive. You might want to stay over."

His thoughts exactly. He could almost thank that jerk Broadstreet and snoopy Sandra Westport for being collective pains in the backside. It gave him just the excuse he was looking for.

"Good idea."

When the elevator doors opened on her floor, she looked up. "Thanks, Nate. You don't have to walk me all the way. Goodbye."

"My grandmother taught me always to see a lady to her door."

"It's really not necessary."

He thought he'd gotten her past nerves, but obviously he'd been wrong. "Please, Katie—let me see you safely to your room. And I won't take no for an answer."

"Okay." She walked quickly down the hall and stopped in front of Room 327. After sliding her key card into the slot, she waited for the blinking green light, then depressed the handle to open the door a crack. "Well, goodbye, Nate. It was good to see you again."

Nervously, she stepped inside and started to close the door. He put his palm up to keep her from shutting it and a flicker of something that looked like fear flashed through her eyes. He dropped his hand. "Wait, Katie. There's something I wanted to ask—"

"Yes?" She met his gaze and the pulse in her throat fluttered wildly. Was she uneasy around him? What had he done to make her so edgy?

"I'm alone."

She looked up and down the hall. "Yeah. I sort of figured that out."

"And you're alone."

"And you know this—how?"

"You told me so earlier—when we were sitting on the bench."

"Right. I forgot," she mumbled. "Do you remember everything?"

When it was as important as her marital status, he did. "I try."

"So, what's your point? I'm sure you have one."

"I do." He ran his fingers through his hair. "The thing is, I hate to eat alone."

"Oh."

She said it as if she hadn't considered the possibility he would ask her to dinner. Definitely not a flirt. With his geek days behind him, aggressive women had been something he'd learned to deal with. He was out of practice with the reluctant kind.

"Would you have dinner with me?"

"I'm pretty tired," she said. Funny, she didn't even pretend to think about it.

"We could order room service. Your room or mine," he suggested.

Instantly she tensed. "I don't think that's a good idea."

He'd thought it an excellent idea. But the expression on her face backed up her statement. He remembered her looking like that the night she'd broken up with Ted Hawkins. Pale and shaken and afraid.

"Okay," he said, unwilling to push. "We can talk tomorrow."

"Maybe," she said vaguely. "Goodbye, Nate."

He frowned at the closed door. There was something very wrong with her and he couldn't shake the feeling that Katie Price had scars on her soul even more harmful than the ones on her face. Which was why he was determined not to let her push him away.

He wouldn't give up on her.

Chapter Three

Kathryn sat in one of the two chairs at the small circular table in front of her window and sipped her morning coffee. Her room had a view of the clock tower at Saunders University. The spire pushing through the thicket of trees was like a sentinel. Or a lone survivor. Like her.

She loved mornings and had felt that way even after the accident, when her life was nothing but a series of question marks. Would she survive? Would she walk again? Without a limp? Would she be scarred forever? Now she knew the answers: yes, yes, almost, and yes.

The miracle workers at the rehabilitation hospital had done their best to get her back on her feet and as close to her pre-accident appearance as possible. It had been months before she'd been pushed out of the rehab nest with a hearty "fly, be free." And now her life was only a single question mark, but it was a doozy. Now what?

The summons from Professor Harrison had enabled her to put the answer aside. And she was relieved, which probably made her a coward. And she hated that she was. She hated being weak. But she was trying to face facts. And the fact was, she was glad to put off a decision about her future. Besides, she genuinely wanted to do what she could for the professor. She could manage to stay at the hotel for a few days and hope to meet with the board of directors to give her testimonial. Then, because her modeling career had come to a screeching halt, she had to figure out what she was going to be when she grew up.

For the moment, she was stuck in her room with no place to go, even if she wanted to. Which she didn't. After yesterday, she had to conclude that she was very bad at slipping in and out of places unseen. Although the silver lining had been running into Nate. Just thinking his name turned the silver lining into a warm glow centered deep in her midsection.

For all the good it did her.

Yesterday she'd shut the poor man down faster than an airport on high alert. That was something the accident hadn't changed. Once a social geek, always a social geek. What had happened in college just intensified the condition. Her agent had given her the lecture about career success depending on being seen and photographed with the right people if she wanted to make it to the top. That had been just before she'd hit life's rock bottom. Her agent hadn't dumped her, but then he didn't have to. No one was calling with work for a face that looked like hers. She'd only had one offer and she'd turned it down.

So she'd never flexed her social muscles and on some level that had been a relief. But poor Nate. He'd been on the receiving end of her nerdiness and was probably out counting his lucky stars while doing the dance of joy that she'd saved him from himself.

A knock on her door startled her. She wasn't expecting anyone.

She stood and walked over to look through the peephole. Surprise mixed with pleasure when she recognized Nate. She waited for uneasiness, and was a little amazed when it never came. Instead, she was grateful that he hadn't washed his hands of her.

She removed the chain lock and opened the door. "Hello."

"Good morning." He studied her. "You look well rested."

She winced inwardly even though his tone was nothing but friendly. But she knew he was needling her about the transparent way she'd turned down his invitation. And she deserved the teasing. The irony was that she liked him. Way to make him like her back, she thought. But she'd learned the hard way that familiarity breeds contempt. And it worked both ways. The more he learned about her, the more likely he'd be to leave her in the dust.

"I'm fine," she said. "How are you?"

"Never better." He grinned as he leaned a broad shoulder against the door frame and folded his arms across his chest.

Today he was casually dressed in jeans and a sport shirt with a very expensive logo on the front. He'd been pretty devastating in his suit and tie, but this look made her weak in the knees. And that was only one of the reasons she refused to invite him into her room.

"I don't mean to sound blunt—"

"But?" he said. "And before you ask, no one starts out like that unless there's a *but* coming."

"But," she said, struggling not to smile. "What are you doing here?"

"I believe we said we'd talk today."

"Yes. But I thought you were just being nice." With no intention of following through.

"So you think I'm that superficial?"

"I hardly know you well enough to judge. I'm just being realistic."

"Realistic about judging me?" One eyebrow lifted. "Let me see if I've got this right. You don't remember me, but you're making judgments about what I will or won't do."

"You're twisting this like a pretzel."

"Twisting is such an ugly word."

"But accurate," she challenged.

"To be more precise, I'm clarifying."

"I'm not going to debate with you. Obviously you'd win."

"I like winning," he admitted.

"So what are you here to talk about?"

He straightened and slid his fingertips into the pockets of his jeans. "I tracked down Sandra Westport and talked to her on the phone."

"I see. Did you convince her to back off on Professor Harrison?"

He shook his head. "No, but I talked her into having lunch with me so I could do that."

"Good luck."

"I could use some. Not to mention backup," he said, giving her a pointed look.

"Me?"

He nodded. "Yeah. She might feel less threatened if there was another woman present. I'd rather not look like the big bad bully."

"I couldn't," she said automatically.

"True. No one would ever mistake you for a bully."

"No. I meant I couldn't possibly go with you."

He shook his head. "Technically, that's not true. I'll drive. All you have to do is sit in the passenger seat. We meet Sandra at the restaurant, order food and eat. That's exceedingly doable."

"That's not what I meant and you know it."

"Yeah."

"Be serious, Nate."

"I am. About needing some help."

"Not mine. I'm probably the last person Sandra Westport wants to have lunch with." Kathryn had turned down a request from the other woman, only a week or two ago. It was highly unlikely Nate would benefit by her presence at lunch.

"You'd really be doing me a big favor if you'd come along," he insisted.

"What part of *no* don't you understand?" she asked.

"The *N* and the *O*. I'm very fragile," he teased.

There was nothing fragile about him, not in the

way his shirt hugged his muscular biceps or the masculine way he filled out his jeans. But when she looked
closer, for a split second, his eyes showed a hint of
hurt. Then it was gone and she wasn't sure she'd seen
it at all. Just her imagination. She didn't have the
power to wound him. They didn't know each other
well enough. And why in the world would he even
want to get to know her better when he could have his
pick of perfect women? A man with his blow-in-my-
ear-and-I'll-follow-you-anywhere-good-looks would
not be bothered by a rejection from someone who
looked like her.

"Fragile my foot," she blurted out. "This isn't about
you, Nate."

"You think I don't know that?" he asked, suddenly
serious.

"No, I don't think you do."

"Then you'd be wrong. In spite of what you think,
I'm not an insensitive jerk."

"I don't think that—"

"Obviously you do," he interrupted. "In my own defense let me point out that I got it when you hid behind your sunglasses. I'm not so self-absorbed that I
don't get that you've been through something traumatic."

"There's no way you can understand what I'm feeling," she retorted.

"There's that jumping to conclusions thing again.
How can you possibly know what I would or would
not understand?"

"Come on. It's not jumping to conclusions when the
man looks like you." She stared at him. "You belong

in the sexiest lawyer section of *People* magazine's sexiest man of the year issue. You couldn't possibly know what it feels like to look in the mirror and know this is the best you're ever going to look. You can't understand what it feels like when people won't look you in the eye because they see the scars and don't know how to deal with it."

He frowned. "This isn't about other people. It's about you, Katie. You can't sit passively in a room. Life isn't a spectator sport. It happens if you let it."

"You're preaching to the choir, Nate. No one knows better than me that life happens. It happened all over my face and it isn't pretty."

"Now who's twisting words?"

"I'm just saying, until you've walked in my shoes, don't presume to know how I feel."

"And I'm saying things aren't always the way they seem. Have you ever heard that beauty is in the eye of the beholder?"

"That's baloney."

One eyebrow rose. "The Katie I knew wasn't a glass-is-half-empty person."

That arrow sliced clear to her soul and drew blood. "I resent that. It's not pessimism, it's realism."

"You say tomato, I say toe-mah-toe. You say potato—"

"Oh, for Pete's sake."

"No, for mine."

He looked so sincere, and her steadfast resolve began to waver. It had all seemed so simple before he showed up in the flesh. He'd accepted her turndown; she was okay with that. But now, seeing all that attractive flesh, engaging in stimulating verbal sparring, she wasn't sure about anything. Except that suddenly the loneliness she hadn't even acknowledged loomed black and frightening. She hadn't realized how isolated and alone she'd felt since her accident.

He was there and she found his larger-than-life personality so very appealing, so very difficult to resist. Even for her—the ice queen. But she knew not resisting was a prerequisite for disaster. If she made the mistake of letting him close, the ugliness from her past was certain to come out and she simply couldn't bear that after working so hard to bury it.

"Look—" he ran his fingers through his hair "—all I'm trying to say is that you can't stand at a fork in the road indefinitely. Sooner or later you'll get run over."

This time she couldn't suppress a smile. "Don't tell me. Let me guess. You do motivational speaking on the side."

He grinned. "Busted."

"I knew it." That boyish expression combined with his square-jawed, lean good looks, and perseverance and genuine likability propelled her stomach into a triple backflip.

"Actually I'm just a hardworking attorney who's only interested in motivating you to go out with me." Again he twisted and clarified.

"I don't know, Nate."

"I do." He reached out a hand, but didn't touch her. "Look, Katie, whether you believe it or not, I know how to take no for an answer. But I hope I won't have to."

She shook her head. "I just can't go to lunch with you and Sandra."

"Okay. Then how about just me?"

"What? I thought you needed to try and get her to cut the professor some slack."

"That's not what I meant. I'll see Sandra and try to get her to back off. Then we can have dinner tonight. Please?"

No was on the tip of her tongue, but Kathryn hadn't counted on his ability to captivate her. Suddenly she was the one who didn't understand the *N* and the *O*.

"All right. Dinner," she said. "But, Nate, could we—"

"You order room service. I'll be here about seven?"

She nodded. "Seven."

When he was gone she closed her door and leaned against it. How was she grateful? She mentally ticked off the ways. He was sensitive to her need for privacy with these baby steps forward. But he didn't know some of her hesitation was because this was her first step with a man since that awful night in college. He'd worn down her defenses with his charming verbal assault and she hoped she didn't regret her decision. Still, she trusted him and for the life of her she couldn't explain why.

But she didn't need a mirror to know she was grinning from ear to ear. Defenses be damned. For the first time in a long time she was looking forward to an evening with a very charming and attractive man.

Nate was anticipating dinner with Katie that night and nearly missed the turn for the Italian restaurant where he'd agreed to meet Sandra Westport for lunch. He'd thought getting her phone number would be difficult until he talked to his paralegal, Rachel James. Nate had given her some time off to assist Professor Gilbert in locating a former student who might be able to help save his job at the university. She didn't know it yet, but her time off would be with full pay even though suspicious Sandra had enlisted her support in her crusade for the truth. Whatever that was. At least Rachel had a phone number for the woman.

He parked and went inside, the smell of garlic and spices making his mouth water. Skipping breakfast did that to a guy. When he explained he was meeting someone, the hostess showed him to an outside table where Sandra was already waiting, sipping an iced tea.

While he'd been nosing around Saunders U, he'd seen her. Their paths had crossed in the last couple weeks and fortunately she hadn't remembered him from college. But he couldn't forget the beautiful blond, blue-eyed cheerleader who'd hung out at the Alpha Omega fraternity house with David Westport, her boyfriend. He wondered how much she remembered from that time. Did she know that he'd rigged the house's security cameras to film in the bedrooms? And would the curious woman going after a good man like the professor believe Nate had been duped into using his expertise to do it?

Joining that boys-will-be-boys society was something else he wished he could forget. How in God's name had his past become so littered with regrets? Where was the guy with dreams of using his knowledge and skills for people in trouble who desperately needed it? Officially that's what he did, but only someone in trouble who could afford his exorbitantly high fee. How had he gone so far off his original path?

He pushed the thoughts away and braced for hurricane Sandra. He held out his hand. "Sandra? Nate Williams."

Her eyes widened. "Nate Williams? You loaned me your handkerchief."

"When you were crying," he remembered. "I hope everything is better now."

"Williams," she said. "That's what the *W* was for. I've been calling you Mr. W."

"That works. Thanks for meeting me." He sat.

"Fortunately you caught me on a Friday. The only other days I come into Saunders are Monday and Wednesday."

That was still enough time to do the professor damage, unless he could convince her to abandon her crusade. "Have you already ordered?"

She shook her head. "Not yet. But I know for a fact that the food is great. David and I have eaten here and I highly recommend the pasta primavera. Unless a macho guy like you needs his daily ration of raw meat."

He wondered if the barb indicated she was aware of his high-profile profession. When she didn't say more, he ignored it. And he was grateful she apparently didn't remember that in his fraternity days he was the overweight geek in the corner, hibernating and hoping no one would notice him. These days he always made healthy food choices. It was easier with money. Almost everything was.

"That sounds good to me." He ordered for them, then met her gaze. "How are you and David?"

She looked radiant. "We couldn't be better."

"Tell me about the two of you."

"We have a family. Twins. Molly unfortunately inherited my naturally curly hair and Michael favors David with his black hair."

"That's great. Twins must be a challenge."

"Yes. But I love it. Takes some doing to juggle motherhood with my job at the newspaper. So right now I just do small-town stuff. David coaches Little League and soccer for our kids' teams. Once an athlete, always an athlete. Passing those good physical genes on to the next generation. Although how that translates into Ping-Pong is anyone's guess."

"Excuse me?"

She laughed. "The twins have their hearts set on being the first brother-sister Ping-Pong team in the Olympics."

"Goals are good."

"And to pay for those goals we own a small grocery in the North End of Boston. Which is probably way more information than you wanted." She took a breath. "And what about you?"

"I'm a lawyer. My office isn't far from where your store is."

"So you're an attorney," she said, studying him closely.

"Yes." He tensed, waiting for the "aha" moment. The instant when she recognized him from some press conference for a high-profile case he'd handled or a news segment analyzing his courtroom performance.

He hoped Nickelodeon trumped nightly news in her house. When she didn't say anything, he allowed himself to relax.

"Did you always want to be an attorney?"

He nodded and relaxed a little more. Anyone who really knew him from college would remember that.

"Do you like what you're doing?"

"Do you always ask so many questions?"

She smiled. "It's a reporter thing."

"Is your vendetta against Professor Harrison a reporter thing?" Nate asked.

"It's a reporter's responsibility to search out the truth."

"No matter who gets hurt?"

She sighed. "I look at it like going to the doctor. Sometimes it hurts, but knowing what's going on always brings you peace of mind in the long run."

"I disagree." He didn't want anyone knowing what was really going on with him. Especially Katie. "So, what have you got against the professor?"

Frowning, Sandra leaned forward. "Are you asking specifically? Or just inquiring about my general motivation?"

"Either. Both." Nate lifted one shoulder. "Whatever you want to tell me."

"I'm simply trying to learn the truth."

"Even if it costs him the career he loves? A way of life that's all he has since his wife died?"

"There's something strange going on with him, Nate."

"Define 'something.'"

"I've been digging—"

"From what I hear, you could be halfway to China."

She smiled. "Very funny. The thing is, I'm finding some disturbing patterns in the professor's behavior."

The waiter appeared and set their plates of pasta in front of them. When they were alone again, Nate met her gaze. "What kind of patterns?"

"Let me start with David. He's a gifted athlete, and a very intelligent man—"

"I can see you're not prejudiced," Nate commented, noting the glow of love that sparkled in her blue eyes. A hollow feeling opened wide in the center of his chest because a man like himself could never hope for what she had—love and a family.

She grinned. "Not me. I'm into the facts. The fact is, I love my husband."

"I envy you."

"Don't sidetrack me."

"Okay. So you were saying that David's a rocket scientist," he said, getting back on the subject.

She laughed. "Hardly. But in spite of above-average IQ, in high school he was more interested in sports than learning and no one was more surprised than David when he received a scholarship. There are supposed to be academic standards for those and his grades just weren't high enough."

"How did he get it?"

"Courtesy of a mysterious benefactor."

The professor had mentioned that. "Do you know who this person is?"

"That's what I'm trying to find out. I've come across more records and found some troubling irregularities."

"So what does that have to do with the professor?"

She frowned. "I haven't found a solid link, at least not on paper. But in every instance of an undeserved scholarship or pulling strings in some way, the person involved was mentored by Professor Harrison."

"That's not proof of anything. It's coincidence. Circumstantial."

"Tell me about it. But he's the common denominator. The link to this mysterious patron."

"I don't get it, Sandra. Someone is doing good—like the Lone Ranger—and you're looking to lynch him from the highest tree."

"It's never okay to do the wrong thing, even if it's for the right reason. There are rules and they're meant to be followed. As a lawyer, I'm surprised you'd even question something so basic."

That's because she didn't know him. "As a lawyer I know everything isn't always black and white. There's a lot of gray areas, which is why we've got judges."

She put down her fork and studied him closely. "Hmm."

"What?" he asked sharply.

"You remind me of someone. I thought so the couple times I saw you on campus and I can't shake the feeling now."

Oh, for crying out loud. Did she mean the geek he used to be? Or the high-profile defense attorney he was now? If she remembered either one it was bad news.

"They say everyone has a double."

"I've heard that."

Time to change the subject and one of his favorites was Katie. "Do you remember Kathryn Price?"

Instantly she looked up and frowned. "Do I? College beauty queen. Model on her way to superstardom. Yeah, I remember her."

"What's wrong?"

"David and I decided to start a camp for disadvantaged children."

"Wow."

"Yeah. He felt guilty about that scholarship he didn't deserve, and then wasted. So together we came up with the camp idea to use his strengths and talents as sort of cosmic payback for the gift he once received."

"That's a great idea."

She smiled. "We think so."

"But?" he prompted.

"We need funding to get it off the ground and decided to impose on our college ties with Kathryn Price. I contacted her through her agent to be the celebrity face for our project and get the donations going."

"What happened?"

"She refused." Her mouth pulled tight. "Rachel James got just a glimpse of her here in Saunders."

"Rachel is my paralegal."

"Small world," Sandra said.

"Yeah. So what did she say?"

"She said Kathryn was wearing a scarf covering most of her face."

"And big sunglasses?" he asked.

"Maybe. Rachel didn't mention that. But she said the wind lifted the scarf enough to see there was something wrong with her face."

"So that explains why she turned you down."

"No, it doesn't. Her agent said she refused to even hear the details. So we never got a chance to pitch the idea. I can't help thinking she's turned into a snob."

Anger churned in his gut. "For someone who preaches the truth above everything, you're certainly jumping to conclusions."

She looked surprised. "Oh?"

He leaned forward and rested his hands on the table. "There could be a thousand reasons she turned you down."

"Like what?"

"She's out of the country on a shoot. She doesn't like sports. She doesn't like you or David. She's busy with a hundred other philanthropic projects that are more near and dear to her heart. Like ballet. Or basket weaving. Or sand sculpture."

Sandra looked surprised. "Wow."

Wow, indeed. When did he forget to censor everything that came out of his mouth? He'd learned to do it in college when any slip could result in being the butt of a painful joke. As a lawyer, the health of his career depended on editing his thoughts, words and deeds. But just now, he'd worn his heart on his sleeve. Not smart, Williams, he thought.

"I guess I know where you're coming from," Sandra said.

"You do?"

"Yeah. I'd say that was a typical male reaction to an incredibly beautiful woman."

"Oh." Good. He wasn't busted after all. "The thing is, I ran into Katie—Kathryn. I happen to know she has a good reason for turning you down."

"And what would it be? Surely not sand sculpture," she said wryly.

"No." He laughed sheepishly. "I'm not at liberty to say."

"You know that just makes a reporter more curious and determined."

"I know." Snooping reporters were the bane of his existence. But Katie was none of her business. "All I'll say is that she's fragile and needs a little time. You need to cut her some slack."

He hoped that didn't pique her journalist's curiosity and get her off the professor only to go after Katie. "Look, Sandra, I came here to convince you to leave Professor Harrison alone. He's only ever wanted to help students. I think this witch hunt is wrong after all he's done."

"Wrong has been done, all right. Students who had the credentials to receive those scholarships were victimized. What about justice for them?"

He read the determination in her expression and knew when he was hitting his head against the wall. "So I can't convince you to back off?"

"Not on a bet."

"Okay. Then let me help you."

"Why?" she asked suspiciously.

"So I can prove you're wrong about him. That he didn't do anything improper."

"You're on." She nodded emphatically. "I've got a ton of files to go through. As an attorney, you should be into file minutiae."

"Yeah," he groaned. "I live for the opportunity to look for a needle in a haystack."

"I'll give you a stack to go through. The thing is, Nate," she said sincerely, "if he acted dishonestly, he should pay the price."

"Even if good came out of it? Wrong thing, right reason?"

"It's still wrong."

The pasta primavera settled like a stone in Nate's stomach. Her words felt like an indictment of his own life. He represented felons. Not an especially noble profession. He wasn't the man his grandmother had raised and she wouldn't be proud of what he'd become. He wasn't particularly proud of himself, either, and hadn't been for a long time. It never mattered before, but it did now.

Because of Katie.

Chapter Four

Kathryn glanced at the clock on the desk as she paced back and forth in front of the basic beige couch in her room. It was almost time for her seven o'clock dinner appointment. She refused to call it anything else. Late, late for a very important date. Nate had called her Alice in Wonderland and she was beginning to feel that way. She was late—for life.

This was a cozy room, but it wasn't home. It wasn't surprising that she wasn't anxious to go back to California and not because of the earthquakes. She had no career to go back to. But she had to figure out what to do for the professor as soon as possible because she couldn't afford an indefinite stay in this room.

And speaking of rooms, what had possessed her to

let Nate into her life at all, let alone into her own for dinner?

She hadn't dated since college and it was scary to be with a man at all. Yet she'd agreed to room service! Most women were smart enough to meet men in public places. But with her face scarred, that was scarier than room service. She wasn't quite sure how Nate had talked her into this. He must be one heck of a lawyer.

Now the pressure was on and the timing was tricky. Dinner needed to be here within a few minutes of when he showed up so they wouldn't have too much time alone before room service arrived. But she didn't want it here too early or the cold food ick factor would set in.

Why should she care if the food turned out to be mush? There was a comforting thought. It's not as if there would be anything long-term between them. Her future was up in the air and until she got her act together, there wasn't room for anyone else in this mess she called a life. She couldn't explain why she'd trusted Nate more than anyone in ten years, but that didn't mean she could muster a level of trust that would sustain a lasting relationship.

There was a knock on her door and the butterflies fluttering in her stomach collided and fused into a lump the size of Massachusetts. She took a deep, cleansing breath, then released it as she went to check the peephole. It was Nate, not room service, and she opened the door wide, as her heart gave the inside of her chest the one, two punch.

"Hi, Nate."

His smile was devastatingly attractive. "Katie."

He was the only one who used the nickname and it seemed somehow special, warming her clear to her soul. "Come in."

"Thanks." He handed her a brown bag twisted around a bottle.

Frowning, she said, "What's this?"

"Sparkling water. I couldn't find any in the hotel gift shop, so I went to the convenience store down the street. That's why I'm a little late."

Relief washed over her at the same time she was ashamed of herself. She'd been so sure it was some kind of liquor to get her drunk. There it was—her failure to trust. Proof positive of her faith-in-men handicap. But she didn't have to trust him forever, just tonight. Dinner. That was all. He'd get tired of looking at her flawed face and failure to attain intimacy, then an F16 flying Mach one couldn't get him out of there fast enough. She was silly to even consider a future and Nate in the same thought process.

"Thanks. That was sweet of you." She took the bag. "I'm sorry. Dinner was supposed to be here by now."

He glanced around. "I'm shocked and appalled."

"Room service isn't that reliable."

"Not room service. I thought you'd whip something up with a curling iron, a blow-dryer and a hot plate."

She laughed. "Don't think I couldn't. But I'm fresh out of hot plates so I had to rely on hotel staff and, as you can see, dinner hasn't arrived."

A small smile curved his mouth as he stared at her. "I hadn't noticed. With a beautiful woman like you in the room, I can't even think about food."

It was blatant flattery, probably as transparent as plastic wrap, but her bruised and barren soul soaked it up like a drought-ravaged desert. At the same time she wanted the earth to open and swallow her whole. He made her want to be beautiful. For the first time in ten years. And the thought was heartbreaking. Why did she meet him now, when she'd never be pretty again?

Before that thought had the chance to suck her down, there was a knock at the door. This time Nate answered it and she was grateful he was there.

"Room service," he said after checking, then he opened up for the hotel staff to push the cart inside. "Just set up on the table by the window."

Kathryn stood out of the way and let him handle everything. After a year out of the fast lane, things that had once been second nature, seemed foreign and difficult now. Nate was very good at it.

When the young man finished setting up the table, he held out the check for a signature. She started to take it, but Nate beat her.

"I'll take care of this," he said. He looked at the young man in hotel uniform, with gold name tag pinned to his uniform. "Justin, make sure the charges go on my room."

"Yes, sir."

"Nate. No. That's not right," she protested. "I insisted."

"But it was my idea." He handed the check back to the waiter who glanced at it and smiled broadly. When he was gone, Nate said, "I wanted to take you out to dinner because I wanted to spend some time with you. But more than that, while I was spending my time, I wanted you to be comfortable. So, in reality, this is my thing and we both get what we want. It's a wonderful custom known as compromise."

She tipped her head to the side and studied the determination carved on that strong jaw. "I don't suppose it would do any good to argue?"

His eyes sparkled with humor. "You can if you like. But arguing is what I do best. It's how I make my living. I research facts, precedents, cases and anything else I can come up with. Then I argue in front of a judge and jury. So I'm experienced and if I do say so myself, I'm pretty good at it. Consider yourself warned. If you still want to argue—" he bent at the waist and held out his hand "—be my guest."

She laughed and wondered how he made her do that. In the last twenty-four hours it felt as if she'd laughed more than the previous ten years. But it felt so good, so cleansing that she simply let the feeling wash over her.

"Okay, counselor. You win. But I guess you knew that since you hear it all the time."

"Thank you. You're very gracious in defeat." He went to the table and pulled out a chair. "Now, your feast awaits, my lady."

When she was seated, he settled himself in the chair across from her and lifted the metal lids from the plates. She'd pre-ordered for the two of them. Pasta primavera, garlic rolls—always a line of defense if things moved in a way she wasn't comfortable with—and antipasto salad. This was something she liked and also one of the least expensive entrées on the room service menu. Although thanks to Nate that hadn't been a problem.

"I hope you like it," she said.

He smiled. "Looks great. I'm starved."

"Me, too." She picked up her fork and realized it was true. As a model, she'd always struggled to keep her weight down, then after the accident, it hadn't been a problem since she had little or no appetite. Tonight she was ravenous. It was as if, baby step by baby step, Nate was bringing her back to life. And she wasn't sure she liked it.

"So where did you and Sandra Westport have lunch today?"

"Some Italian place just off campus," he said.

"Was it nice?"

"Very."

"How was the food?"

"Excellent. But the company wasn't nearly as good." He met her gaze and winked.

"What did you have?"

He hesitated. "Why do you want to know?"

"Just making conversation." She'd been eating with gusto and wiped some sauce from the corner of her mouth. "I'm enjoying this more than anything I've had in a long time so I guess I'm just into talking about food."

"Oh."

"So what was lunch?"

"Some Italian dish," he said vaguely.

"No kidding. At an Italian place? Who'd have guessed?"

He held his fork over his plate as he looked at her. "Is that sass? Are you making fun of me?"

"Yes."

"Oh."

She frowned. "What's wrong?"

"I was sort of hoping that was flirting."

She thought about that for a moment. "I suppose there's a fine philosophical line between sassing and flirting. But it was definitely sass, because I never flirt."

"Never?" he asked, eyebrow lifting hopefully.

"Never." She made it a point not to encourage attention from men. Nate was simply more persistent than most.

He lifted one broad shoulder in a shrug. "One man's sass is another man's flirt."

"Are you always a glass-is-half-full kind of guy?"

"No. Just with you."

Now that was flirting. But she wasn't about to say so because the compliment warmed her from head to toe and inside out. She could only hope the flush she felt on her cheeks wasn't noticeable to anyone but her. Time to change the subject. She looked down at her half-eaten pasta. "So, you managed to sidestep my question. You never told me what you had for lunch."

He shook his head ruefully. "For the record I'm grateful you're not an attorney I'd have to face in the courtroom."

"For the record, you're very good at changing the subject."

"You're not going to let this drop, are you?"

She shook her head. "For some reason you don't want to tell me and that makes me awfully curious."

"Okay. I had pasta primavera."

"Oh, Nate. We could have ordered another entrée. Why didn't you tell me?"

"Because you'd feel bad. And I didn't want you to." He put down his fork and reached his hand across the table to cover hers, giving it a warm, reassuring squeeze. "The food is unimportant. It's the company that makes a meal. And yours is the best I've had in…" He thought for a moment, then said, "Longer than I can remember."

"For me, too." And she meant that sincerely. But this conversation had taken an intimate turn that made her acutely uncomfortable. She pulled her hand from beneath his. "So, did Sandra Westport agree to cut the professor some slack?"

"No. Actually, I agreed to help her go through some files."

"You're ratting the professor out?" she asked, surprised.

He shook his head. "If you can't beat 'em, join 'em. Somehow she got hold of a stack of information. Research is the hallmark of a lawyer's job so I told her I'd go through the files. I don't expect to find anything and lack of proof should build a case that Professor Harrison is innocent of any wrongdoing."

"Can I help?" she asked, before she could activate the filter between her brain and mouth.

He smiled. "I'd love the company."

When they were finished eating, he wheeled the room service cart filled with plates and glasses out into the hall and called for pickup. Then he collected the files from his room and spread them out on the small table in front of the couch.

"What am I looking for?" she asked.

He thought for a moment. "Anything that references scholarships, gifts, anywhere his name appears, or the names of the students he contacted to return for a testimonial. I got a list from Rachel James—"

"Who?"

"She's my paralegal, and was a student at Saunders when we were here."

"I don't think I remember her, either."

"Then I shouldn't be offended?" He grinned.

She barely resisted a sigh, knowing she could easily lose herself in the warmth and appeal of that smile. "No. Don't feel bad. There are a lot of students I don't remember."

He frowned at the stack of paperwork in front of him. "And there are a lot of students in here."

"Then we'd better get to work."

Hours later, Kathryn left the room to freshen up after her eyes started to cross and her head pound. When she came back, Nate was sound asleep on her sofa. Now what? Should she wake him and send him to his room? Like a little boy? He was hardly that, she thought, studying him.

He looked younger in sleep, more relaxed. As she studied his face, she noticed two small marks, like scars from chicken pox. She'd never noticed them before and he gave the impression of perfection. She'd never thought in terms of flawlessness until after her accident. How shallow was that? But she was reminded that no one is perfect. And this man was fascinating. As she spent time in his company, more of his interesting facets caught the light and attracted her.

And there was her problem. She was attracted to him and his looks were secondary.

When he moaned in his sleep, her gaze slid to his firm, well-shaped lips. Heat flooded her at the thought of kissing him. What would it be like? And that was new. Temptation was something she hadn't experienced in a long time. It was a dangerous path to contemplate, a trail filled with booby traps. But for some reason she couldn't look away. Probably because it was safe while he slept. And because something about this sleeping man tweaked her memory. But the harder she thought about it, the more elusive the memory.

She yawned and realized how exhausted she was. She eased his head onto a pillow and carefully lifted his long legs onto the couch, stretching them out more comfortably. When he hardly stirred, she realized he was completely worn out, too. What could it hurt to let him sleep there undisturbed?

Nate sat up out of a deep sleep and struggled to remember where he was. On a couch he realized, glancing around as he felt a twinge in his back. He spotted a charmingly feminine pink sweater carelessly tossed over a chair back and he knew right away.

Katie.

Swinging his legs around so he could put his feet on the floor, he winced with embarrassment when it hit him that he'd fallen asleep. Way to win friends and influence the woman he'd never quite been able to forget.

He heard a sound from the bedroom, just before a scream. Adrenaline pumped through him, instantly ripping apart the web of sleep. He raced to her side and sat on the bed where Katie was thrashing and moaning.

"Katie," he said gently, reaching out to touch her shoulder, to let her know he was there.

"No," she said, tossing her head from side to side. "Don't."

"Katie?" He cupped her cheek in his palm. "It's me—Nate."

There was no response except agitated mumbling as she jerked away from his touch. She was having a nightmare. He didn't want to startle her, but he needed to snap her out of it.

He put his palms down on either side of her as he leaned in close and said, "Katie. It's all right."

Her eyes opened and she tried to sit up but his hands on the blankets hemmed her in. When she couldn't move, she started pushing at him, screaming, "No! No!"

He straightened and lifted his hands from the bed, freeing her. Then he reached over and switched the bedside light on so she could see she was safe. Unfortunately, it only underscored the fear in her brown eyes. Her terror tore at his heart. When she sat up, he started to pull her into his arms.

"No. No. Don't touch me." She pushed at his chest, clawing to be free.

When he released her, she scrambled back. Only the wall stopped her retreat.

"You're all right, Katie. It's me. Nate. You're safe."

He kept repeating the same words over and over in a voice as void of emotion as he could make it. And the effort cost him. Because he was feeling a lot—confusion, anger at whoever or whatever had made her frightened, frustration at being unable to comfort her.

"Katie, honey. Relax. Please. You're okay. No one's going to hurt you. I'm here. I won't let anything happen to you. It's Nate."

Finally her eyes seemed to focus. "Nate?"

"Yeah." He let out a long breath. "You were having a nightmare."

Tears he hadn't noticed until now trickled down her cheeks. The need to comfort and protect her overwhelmed him and he reached out, but the flicker of fear in her eyes made him hesitate.

"Katie, let me hold you."

He swallowed hard as he looked at her pink, silky nightgown with the thin straps, revealing as much as it concealed. Ignoring the flare of heat, he slid forward and put his hand on her arm. Her skin was smooth and silky to his touch. When she didn't flinch away, he curved the fingers of his other hand around her upper arm and gently urged her toward him. Her resistance melted away and she relaxed into him. That was the good news. The bad—she started to sob.

He pulled her into his lap and folded her in his arms as she buried her face against his neck. He felt her hot tears wetting his skin and the collar of his shirt.

"It's okay, sweetheart," he whispered soothingly. "Let it out."

Whatever "it" was. Something was going on with her and he wanted to know what. But he was no shrink and he guessed pushing her wasn't the best idea. Not when she was so upset.

He lost track of time as he sat with her. When she was calmer, he was simply grateful to have an excuse to hold her and he knew he was going to hell for the selfish thought. The truth was, he'd never touch her again if he could take away whatever demons stalked her. And he knew she had them. The intensity of her nightmare was proof of that.

Then, in spite of his best intentions, he became acutely aware of her soft curves pressed against him. He looked down and his gaze settled on her full lips. His skin grew hot and his blood heated, but he would do his best to hide his reaction from her. For as long as he could remember he'd wanted to kiss Kathryn Price. When had he become such a bastard that he could think about that at a time like this?

Finally she released a cleansing breath and shifted away without sliding off his lap. "I'm sorry, Nate."

"There's nothing to be sorry about. I'm glad I was here."

"Me, too," she said, meeting his gaze.

Her mouth was inches away from his own and he wanted to kiss her more than he wanted his next breath. But this was the wrong place and time.

"The thing is, Nate, I need you. I need a friend."

His heart soared, then took a nosedive. Not only was this the wrong time, her words convinced him there would never be a right one. Friends was the best he could ever hope for. But he shouldn't have expected more than that. Ironically, when his face was scarred and his nose angled a few degrees off center, he'd been good enough for her. His lucrative law practice had allowed him to fix the outside, but left too many scars on his soul. And he would do whatever it took to keep her from seeing them.

"Friends are good," he said, hiding the effort it took to keep his tone light.

She slid off his lap and reached for her lightweight pink terry cloth robe on the end of the bed. When she was primly covered from neck to knee, she said, "I feel comfortable with you. Your bad luck," she said.

Her tone was self-mocking, but he admired her courage in attempting humor when she was clearly troubled and possibly in shock. "My luck has never been better."

She flashed the ghost of a smile. "I think it's time I told you what happened to me."

If anything her skin paled even more, increasing his level of concern for her. "You don't have to, not if it's going to upset you more."

"No. I need to tell you how this happened," she said, her fingers fluttering over the scars on her face.

"Okay. I'm listening."

"It was a car accident. I was hit by a drunk driver."

His chest tightened as rage roared through him. He didn't know what to say so he remained silent.

"I was out celebrating. My agent had called earlier that day to let me know I'd been hired for the assignment that would make my career—one of the major cosmetics companies wanted me for their new ad campaign. My girlfriends took me out to lunch."

"Oh, Katie—" Now he really didn't know what to say. The man who spun words like golden threads was speechless. He'd argued important cases in front of court TV cameras without batting an eye, but he didn't trust himself to keep his emotions in check. Not where she was concerned.

"On the way home, a car crossed over into my lane and hit me practically head-on. My leg was shattered and you can see what it did to my face—flying glass and my sunglasses cut my cheek. I was in the hospital for weeks, then in rehab while I had physical therapy for my leg. Plus numerous surgeries on my face. All the king's horses and all the king's men, couldn't put Kathryn Price together—"

"I hope the son of a bitch who hit you rots in hell." Nate's voice was hard as steel.

"I don't know about the hereafter, but he's doing jail time."

"Good." It was a good thing the creep hadn't approached *him* about legal representation. He couldn't be responsible for helping anyone who'd hurt her. He couldn't be held responsible for kicking the guy's ass.

"The thing is," she said, sitting down beside him on the bed, "from the time I was a little girl, my folks always told me it was a good thing I was pretty because I was behind the barn door when brains were passed out."

"That's ridiculous. You're one of the brightest women—or men for that matter—I know."

"You don't have to say that. I know what my limitations are. And besides, it feels true. The smartest thing I could do was use the assets the Good Lord gave me. And that was my looks." Her top lip trembled and she caught it between her teeth.

"You're still a beautiful woman," he protested, covering her hands with his own.

She shook her head. "The plastic surgeon did everything possible to minimize the scarring. But I had to deal with the reality that no one will hire a face like mine." She met his gaze, then her own skittered away. "I'm not feeling sorry for myself. Heaven forbid. Just being realistic. This is the best I'll ever be."

Her words tugged at him and echoed inside him to a place that hadn't been touched in a long time. In fact, it was a spot he was afraid only she could reach. All he knew was that, whether she would admit it or not, she was still hurting and he wanted to make it better.

He reached out and rested his knuckle beneath her chin, nudging it up so she'd meet his gaze. "Your best is pretty damn special."

And before he could stop himself, he lowered his mouth to hers.

Chapter Five

Kathryn was surprised she recognized that Nate was going to kiss her, but she did—seconds before he did. When she felt his mouth on hers, she couldn't breathe—and not in a good way. He was big and broad and she felt trapped. It was just like ten years ago. Panic welled inside her with a will of its own and rational thought was no match for it.

A black haze of fear enveloped her. She was alone with him and he was so much stronger than she; he could make her do whatever he wanted and she couldn't stop him. Not again; it couldn't be happening again.

She pushed against his chest and instantly he drew back, but she jumped up, her chest heaving as if she'd run a marathon.

"Katie?" He stood, but didn't move away from the bed.

The bed. Her eyes darted to it and memories flashed through her mind, images of being held down and hurt and violated. Memories of being powerless to stop what was happening to her. Memories of self-loathing and recrimination and feeling dirty, so dirty she couldn't bathe long enough or hard enough to ever feel clean again.

She wanted to run, but couldn't take her eyes off him. He'd grab her from behind. She couldn't defend against an attack she couldn't see, if she could protect herself at all. So she backed away from him slowly.

Cold sweat beaded on her forehead and trickled between her breasts. To keep her teeth from chattering, she clamped her jaw shut. Nervously she glanced around the bedroom. She was trapped in here. There was no escape. Without a word, she turned and dashed into the sitting area of her room where she could see the door.

"Katie, what's wrong?"

Nate followed slowly and carefully kept his distance. When she met his gaze, there was hurt along with the confusion. "Kate? It's all right."

How could he say that? Nothing was all right. But his voice, deep and gentle, somehow penetrated her panic. He stood where he was, giving her space and slowly the pounding in her chest slowed. As she calmed, it all became so much worse because she was aware of what she'd done and how she must look. If only the earth would open and swallow her whole. This was why she'd avoided the dating scene all these years. She'd picked the wrong man in college. Because of that error in judgment, she couldn't be alone with a nice man like Nate.

He'd done nothing but kiss her. Scarred face and all, he'd kissed her. And she'd made him feel like America's Most Wanted.

She hated Ted Hawkins. He'd stolen her trust and she'd never be normal again.

"Talk to me, Katie."

When she lifted her hand she saw that it was trembling as much as her mouth. Her heart caught. She'd enjoyed feeling his mouth against hers for that split second before panic set in.

She was so stupid. She'd known what he was going to do and should have stopped him. But she'd wanted so much to kiss him. More than anything she wanted to enjoy intimacy with a man as if she were a normal woman. She'd thought she could handle it. For God's sake! It had been ten years. She'd thought that shattering experience was firmly in the past where it belonged, but it felt like yesterday all over again.

"Katie, what's wrong?"

She took a deep breath. "I could tell you I'm claustrophobic."

"Are you?"

"No," she said on a sigh.

He looked so appealing, his normally perfect brown hair tousled, as if he'd raked his fingers through it countless times. And the back stuck up like feathers. Fatigue deepened the lines beside his nose and mouth, but instead of detracting from his appeal, he looked solid and steady and mature and so terribly handsome.

And so what? Claustrophobia would be preferable

to what ailed her. He probably thought she was crazy. And who could blame him?

He ran his fingers through his hair. "Katie, I'm sorry. Honestly, I never planned to kiss you."

She knew he was telling the truth. She knew he wasn't a threat; he'd taken no for an answer. But that changed nothing.

"You'd better go."

"Okay.

She turned the dead bolt. "Good night—"

"Wait."

She blinked rapidly to see him through the tears that threatened. No way would she let him see. Kathryn Price was damaged goods inside and out, but she wasn't a crybaby. If she was going to lose it again, this time she'd lose it in private.

"What?"

He moved closer, but not near enough to touch her. How did he know space was just what she needed?

"I'm not leaving until I know you're all right."

She laughed, but without humor it was an ugly sound. "We both know I'm not."

"What can I do?"

"Nothing. And there's nothing to say." That was a lie; she owed him an explanation. Because he'd been so sweet and comforting. And she'd been so glad not to be alone with another bad dream, she'd just bared her soul to Nate about the accident. It was still vivid—the crashing, crunching sound of metal on metal half a second before the pain. She'd seen the drunk driver and his face was burned into her memory. In her nightmares he'd morphed into Ted Hawkins. She might not remember Nate, but coming back to Saunders had certainly stirred up a lot of other memories she'd worked very hard to forget.

Obviously putting it out of her mind was a fantasy. But she simply didn't have the emotional energy to talk about it. What good would it do? Besides, she'd already dumped on him enough.

She pulled the tie of her terrycloth robe tighter. "I'm very tired and I'd like to get some sleep. If you want to help, you can say good-night."

"Good night."

She opened the door. "I'll see you, Nate," she said vaguely.

"When?" He gathered up the files he'd been working on before falling asleep, then stood in the doorway, preventing her from shutting him out.

"I thought you said good-night."

"Yeah, but I didn't mean it. At least not yet," he added. "I want to know when I'm going to see you again."

"Do we have to talk about that now?"

He nodded. "I've had enough brush-offs in my time. 'I'll see you' is a classic. Nebulous enough to not be personal. And non-specific enough that time passes without a commitment."

"I can't think about that now." She tucked a strand of hair behind her ear. "I guess when we figure out what to do for the professor—"

"This isn't about Professor Harrison."

"What is it about?" He couldn't be saying what she thought.

"You and me. Breakfast tomorrow."

She shook her head. "I don't know—"

"You have to eat."

"I know, but—"

"I'll take you out someplace. There's a nice little restaurant close to the campus that makes terrific omelets."

He thought she'd be more comfortable in public? How ironic was that? Public was the last place she wanted to be. The truth was ugly—she wasn't comfortable anywhere. When would he realize she was too much trouble? He should run, not walk to the nearest exit and not look back.

"What are you doing?" she asked.

He sighed. "If you have to ask, I'm not doing it very smoothly."

"What?"

"Trying to make a date."

"I don't need a pity date." Anger welled up inside her, pushing out the last scraps of panic. Why couldn't he simply go? Why was he dragging this out, being sweet and funny—making it more difficult?

He stared at her, a softness she didn't understand in his warm brown eyes. "Pity is the furthest thing from my mind. I didn't kiss you because I felt sorry for you. If I did, we wouldn't be having this conversation."

"Yeah. Right."

"The thing is, Katie, you need to get back into the world. Facing it is easier than worrying about what it will be like when you do face it."

"Arrogance, thy name is Nate. How would a Greek god like you know what I feel? Or what I need."

Righteous anger expanded inside her like a Mylar balloon, pushing out her complicated emotions. It was cleansing and safe and she wanted to hold on to the feeling as long as possible.

Surprisingly, Nate smiled. "I know what you're doing."

"And what's that, Dr. Freud?"

"Hiding behind anger. Guys use it all the time to duck and run. It's the easiest emotion to summon and it suppresses everything else."

"Don't tell me. You're not a shrink but you play one on TV." She put her hands on her hips as she stared at him. "Since when do they teach psychology in law school?"

"You'd be amazed at how emotions play into a jury trial. Perception is everything."

"Tell me about it." She pulled the door open wider. "And how do you perceive this?"

He stepped into the hall. "You'll find I'm not easily discouraged."

"Will I?"

His smile widened and grew more mysterious. "Good night, Katie."

"Do you mean it this time?"

"Sleep well."

She closed and bolted her door, before she had to watch him turn and see his broad back moving away from her. She'd mocked him about being a shrink, but she knew he was right. Trying to maintain control of a situation that was out of her hands. She'd chased him off before he realized she was too much trouble and left on his own.

The abject sadness of that thought made her ache deep inside. It made her wish she wasn't irreparably broken. If a sweetheart of a guy like Nate couldn't get her past her past, she'd never be a normal woman. Never be capable of receiving a simple sweet kiss from a man.

She'd fended off advances from guys in her modeling days, but this was the first time she'd regretted it. Nate probably thought she was a nutcase, but telling him what had made her this way would scare him off just as surely. She hoped and prayed that if she kept it hidden long enough, the ugliness would go away. If not, she was determined not to let it touch Nate. It would remain the scar he couldn't see and would never know about.

And so she would maintain her pride. It would have to be enough.

Nate could have any woman in the world he wanted and that woman wouldn't be her. She was a disfigured has-been who wouldn't make the last page of his little black book. The problem was she genuinely liked him. A very dangerous state of mind. Because hope wasn't her friend. Once upon a time she'd hoped to look like she had before the accident. She'd hoped all the king's horses and all the king's men could put Humpty Dumpty back together. And the doctors did all that they could. But she'd never look her best again.

Hope had let her down. And unlike a photograph for a magazine cover, life couldn't be airbrushed. A clean break from him now was just what the doctor ordered.

She couldn't bear it if hope let her down again. Not with Nate.

* * *

Nate was tired, but keyed up and unable to sit still. He couldn't stop thinking about Katie's reaction last night. At the rate he was pacing back and forth, his room would need the carpet replaced before Sandra Westport arrived. She'd offered to swing by the hotel and pick up the damn files. He wished he could blame them for kissing Katie, but the decision had been all his.

He hadn't meant to do it. The problem was he'd fantasized about kissing her in college, and how often did a guy get a second chance? Hell, he'd never had a first chance with her then. He'd never have risked her laughing at him ten years ago. To get that close to his dream girl... His self-control switch had simply malfunctioned.

Unfortunately, now he couldn't stop thinking about the shattered expression in her eyes when she'd pushed him away. Like an animal with fight-or-flight instincts. She'd been ready to do either—or both. Something had happened to her and he didn't mean the accident. She was frightened.

As if it were yesterday, Nate remembered another night she was upset and had left the Alpha Omega house in tears. He'd followed and tried to comfort her, but all she'd said was that she and Ted Hawkins had broken up. Nate had always despised the guy and didn't get what she saw in him. And punching the creep that night was the last fulfilling thing Nate could remember doing. He'd done it because Ted had made Katie cry.

But Nate knew he'd turned into a man who could

hurt her and he'd rather cut off his right arm than do her any more harm. He had to beef up his restraint around her, because acting on his feelings would be one more sin to add to a growing list. And hurting her would be the most unforgivable of all.

He was so deep into his thoughts, the knock on the door startled him. When he opened it, Sandra Westport stood there, looking lovely in a white, thin-strapped sundress, sunglasses perched like a headband in her hair. Nate thought again that David Westport was a lucky man.

"Hi," she said, keys in hand.

"Hi, yourself." He pointed to the box of files on the floor. "That was a colossal waste of time. I found nothing incriminating."

She rested a hand on her hip. "Would you tell me if you did?"

"Of course."

"Really? Loyalty to Professor Harrison wouldn't prevent you from revealing anything dishonest?"

"I owe him a lot," Nate admitted.

"Like what?"

"For one thing, tutoring."

"I thought you were smart," she said, frowning.

He grinned. "Translation—brainer geek."

"Well, yeah." She looked sheepish.

"If the shoe fits…" He held out his hand to indicate she should take a seat in the chair.

"This must be good." She walked in and sat down, her purse in her lap.

When he was settled on the sofa across from her, he met her gaze. "That was a tough year for me. I missed a lot of classes. Family problems. But you know class absence can significantly lower your grade. I needed to ace the finals in those English classes to keep from being kicked out of school."

"So the professor helped?"

He noticed the suspicious look on her face. "It's not what you're thinking."

"And that would be?" she asked, arching an eyebrow.

"That he gave me the test ahead of time. But you'd be wrong. He condensed his class lectures and made me work to make up what I'd missed."

"And?"

"I did well on the finals. Not only did I get off academic probation, it made the difference between getting a law degree from one of the best universities as opposed to a so-so school."

"I see."

"The thing is, part of it was my own fault. But the professor didn't hold that against me."

"What was your fault?" she asked.

"I was approached to join the fraternity." He'd been thinking about it just before she'd arrived, and the undissolved knot in his chest hardened like a stone.

"If family issues were so time-consuming, why did you join a fraternity?"

"My grandmother encouraged me to." He rested his elbows on his knees and linked his fingers. "She was worried about me. Because—" he met her gaze "—I had no friends."

"You?" she asked, obviously surprised. "Don't take this the wrong way, but a guy who looks like you would have more friends, and I'm talking of the female persuasion, than you could count."

"I didn't look like this—then. In college I wasn't as fit and—"

She snapped her fingers. "I remember now. David and I used to hang out at the fraternity house. You were that pudgy guy." She studied him intently. "Didn't you have scars on your face?"

The knot in his chest tightened. "Yeah."

"And a broken nose?"

"Guilty as charged," he said ruefully.

"Speaking of guilt…" Her gaze narrowed. "Aren't you the one who wired the fraternity house with cameras."

"That's me."

"And what about the ones in the bedrooms?" she accused.

"I was told it was all about security."

"That's pretty naive."

"That's being charitable." He hadn't expected understanding from suspicious Sandra Westport. The truth was he didn't deserve her sympathy or understanding. He'd been a dope. "I wanted to fit in." He shrugged. "And they wanted to exploit my expertise."

"And they did." She frowned. "Did you know about the sex videos?"

"Eventually. I was already in law school when the guys responsible were expelled for sexual misconduct. I figured that was poetic justice."

"Ted Hawkins was gone by then, too. But there was some a fraternity reunion and he bragged about having a tape of Kathryn Price."

Nate's blood ran cold. "I hadn't heard that."

"It was right around the time her career started to take off. She was making entertainment news as the rising star in the modeling world."

"Ted Hawkins is a son of a bitch."

Her blue eyes widened. "Good Lord. Now I know who you are."

It was too much to hope he could fly under her radar indefinitely. But about the same time he'd lost his naiveté, bluffing had become his middle name and he had to try. "Who am I?"

"*The* Nate Williams." She tsk-tsked. "You were defense counsel in that high-profile murder trial several years ago. The husband was accused. All circumstantial evidence. Tell me I'm wrong," she challenged.

If only he could, he thought, and sighed. "That's me."

"I can't believe I didn't recognize you right away. It must be all this business with the professor. If I wasn't so distracted, I'd have picked up on it sooner." She pointed at him. "Oh my God. Didn't you defend Ted Hawkins just recently? It was all over the news that you lost the case."

"Yeah. Guilty again."

"There was a lot in the press about the great Nate Williams losing his edge."

He stood and walked over to the window, staring out at Saunders U in the distance. Had he lost his killer instinct? He hadn't wanted Ted's case in the first place. Especially when he was in career crisis mode. But the frat brother connection had compelled him to take it on. That and pressure from his law firm partners to represent the publicity-generating real estate developer.

Growing up poor and picked on, Nate had always pictured himself the champion of the underdog. He'd never envisioned himself the lawyer who took on cases for the billable hours. But the lucrative opportunities were hard to ignore. Somewhere on his journey to idealism he'd taken a wrong turn to cynicism. And his skepticism grew as he played his part in freeing felons to offend again.

"I can't believe Nate Williams, hotshot high-profile attorney is the same guy from college who couldn't keep his eyes off Kathryn Price."

He winced and turned back to her. "Was I that obvious?"

"No. Just a guess," she said, giving him a "gotcha" look. "But an educated one. When we had lunch, and her name came up, you had a definite protective thing going on."

"So I am that obvious."

"Noticing something like that is a chick thing. Maybe a reporter thing, too," she explained. Then she frowned. "Does she know you defended her old boyfriend?"

If she did, it wasn't obvious. And he would give up the corner office and great view to keep it from her.

He looked at Sandra. "Look, I need to ask you a favor."

"Oh?" A glint stole into her eyes.

"It's about Katie—Kathryn Price."

"I figured."

"She's here. At the hotel."

"Really?"

"Yeah. I ran into her a couple days ago. She didn't recognize me, either. The thing is, I don't want her to remember me from college."

"Oh?"

"It wasn't my finest hour." Not entirely true. It was better than most of the hours he'd put in since.

"I like to think we've all changed for the better," she said generously.

"We've changed, all right."

Maybe she was better; he'd only gone downhill. In spite of that, maybe luck was on his side and he had a chance for a do-over. The geeky guy bumping along that rough college road was gone and this was the opportunity he'd never had ten years ago to spend some time with Katie Price.

"I guess you've got your reasons for not wanting her to remember you." Her eyebrow arched. "I've got a proposition for you."

"I smell a negotiation coming on." Now he was on familiar ground. Bargaining was an attorney's bread and butter.

"I won't pursue busting you if you'll use your powers of persuasion for good."

"Define 'good.'"

"Convince Kathryn Price to be the celebrity spokeswoman for the children's sports camp David and I are starting." Before he could interrupt, she hurried on. "The thing is, we need funding. We need someone to be the recognizable face for our cause. I hate imposing on past acquaintances, but she's the only celebrity I know."

Long shot didn't begin to describe the odds of success. He couldn't even convince Katie to go out in public. Although wild horses couldn't drag that info out of him when Sandra was holding all the cards. He'd learned to play his own cards close to the vest and practicing law had only intensified the lesson.

But he wouldn't lie. That never was or would be his style. "I think it would be good for her," he hedged.

Sandra smiled teasingly. "If you'll convince her to do it, I'll keep your secret."

"There are too many already," he mumbled. Then he met her gaze. "I'll mention it, but you need to know I won't try to sway her one way or the other. That's a decision she needs to make without pressure or persuasion."

Sandra stood to leave. "Okay. I'll keep your secret anyway."

"Thanks," he said as she picked up the box of files. "Why?"

"You're welcome. And let's just call it a reward for going through these tedious records. By the way, I choose to believe you're telling the truth about finding nothing incriminating."

"I'm a lot of things, but a liar isn't one of them."

"Well, someone is a liar. And I'll get to the truth," she vowed, on her way out the door.

When she was gone, Nate realized he'd just dodged a bullet. He wasn't sure whether or not he'd lost his edge in the courtroom, but his negotiating skills were apparently sharp enough to persuade the persistent journalist to keep his identity hush-hush. He'd meant it when he'd said there were too many secrets. And a lot of them were his—his past, his present and his growing feelings for Katie Price were all things he wanted to keep top secret.

Chapter Six

"At least my hair is still the same."

Kathryn clicked the blow-dryer back into its cradle, then fluffed her shoulder-length hair as she looked at herself in the mirror above her vanity. She was still learning to live with the scars. The shrink at the physical rehabilitation hospital advised her to focus on the positive and her thick shiny brown hair was positively her best feature now. Because the scars were still visible even after applying makeup with all the skill she'd acquired in her modeling days. In her jeans and white cotton blouse, she looked as good as she possibly could.

"I'm all dressed up and have no place to go." She sighed, then walked into the living area to figure out what she would do for breakfast.

When the phone rang, she walked over to the desk and picked it up. "Hello?"

"Hi, Katie."

No one but Nate called her that. The sound of his deep voice, a little rusty first thing in the morning, sent her stomach plunging as if she'd just jumped from an airplane for her first skydive. She hadn't seen him since the night before last when she'd freaked out about his kiss and figured he'd washed his hands of her. Then she'd tried to convince herself she was relieved about it. The glow currently spreading through her midsection was proof that she'd been lying to herself.

"Hello, Nate."

"Did you sleep well?"

As opposed to being awakened by a bad dream like the other night. Her cheeks heated with mortification when she remembered everything that followed. "Yes, thanks. And you?"

"Fine."

There was an awkward silence. "So. Why did you call?" she asked.

"Are you decent?"

"By that I assume you mean up and dressed as opposed to well mannered and respectable."

"I do." There was a smile in his voice.

"Yes, I'm decent. Why?"

"Open your door."

"What? To my room?"

"Yes."

She looked through the peephole, then did as he instructed because he was standing there. Her heart stuttered at the sight of him in an expensive pale yellow shirt and loafers paired with worn jeans. He was a sight for sore eyes and so handsome her breathing caught, forcing her to kick-start it again by pulling air deep into her lungs.

"Why didn't you just knock?" she asked.

He flipped his cell phone closed. "Just testing the waters."

She folded her arms over her chest. He was announcing himself so she wouldn't feel threatened. How sweet was he? She hated that she'd made him feel he had to do that.

"You couldn't possibly think I'm mad at you."

"Yeah. I could. I have this pesky aggressive streak. And this may surprise you, but I've been told I have a problem taking no for an answer."

She pressed her lips together for a moment to suppress a grin. "I'm not mad."

"Does that mean you're not unhappy to see me and I can invite you to breakfast? If you haven't eaten, that is."

"I haven't. But—"

"Don't say it." He leaned a broad shoulder against the doorjamb and crossed his arms over his wide chest. "*But* has got to be the most offensive word in the English language."

"Nate, I don't think I'm ready for the general public to see my scars."

He frowned. "Did you go out at all yesterday?"

"What does that have to do with anything?" she asked turning away.

"The witness is nonresponsive. Answering a question with a question is classic avoidance technique."

"I'm not on trial. And fresh air is highly overrated," she said defensively.

"So you were cooped up here all day? You should have called me," he said, not even waiting for her to confirm his suspicions.

"You don't need to entertain me. I can take care of myself. And, believe it or not, I can handle the pitying glances and curious stares. That's not why I'm keeping a low profile."

"Then why?"

She sighed. "Somewhere out there is a greedy photographer who's just waiting to get his 'money' shot."

"First picture of Kathryn Price post-accident," he said.

"I'm glad you get it." Behind her she heard the door click closed and winced. She'd lost count of the number of times she'd rejected him. She didn't blame him for leaving without a word.

Then she felt movement behind her and the warmth of his body just before he turned her toward him, crooking his finger under her chin to nudge it up. When she met his gaze, he said, "If I've said this before, I apologize for the repetition. You can't hide forever."

Her heart hammered against the inside of her chest as she stared into his face—so kind, so understanding, so supportive. So perfect. There was no way he could completely get how she felt.

"Look, Nate, I know sooner or later I'll have to get out there. But when I do someone is going to take my picture and sell it to the highest bidding tabloid who will put the sleaziest spin on the story."

"I'd be happy to sue them for you."

She shook her head. "The problem is when I'm out in the open, I'm part of the public domain. There was a case recently where a photographer took a picture of a major star's home from a helicopter over the ocean. She sued to keep him from publishing the photos and lost. Not only that, she had to pay all his legal costs. You probably remember it."

"Yeah. Judges get pretty cranky when First Amendment rights are involved."

"The thing is, I'll do it in my own time, my own way. When I'm ready to go out there."

He nodded. "Okay."

"It's not that I don't appreciate the invitation," she added quickly as she walked over to the door and put her hand on the knob. "I really do. I hope you have a lovely breakfast."

"I intend to."

He picked up the phone on her desk and punched a button. "This is Nate Williams. I'd like to order room service sent to room 327 and billed to my room, number 329."

He's next door, she thought. They had a connecting door. And he still called to give her a heads-up that he was outside her room. She wondered how this amazing-looking guy had developed a hypersensitive soul. More important, she realized, he wasn't leaving. The glow his phone voice produced smoldered inside her, threatening to send her up in flame. This was bad. Every time she saw him and he did something ultra-sweet, she was sucked in a little more. Maybe it would be better if he walked away—now, before she was in too deep. But it wasn't that simple because her next thought was that she couldn't help being glad he hadn't given up on her.

She sighed and figured she had no choice but to share breakfast with the man who refused to take no for an answer.

A short time later they'd finished eating and were lingering over coffee at the small table for two by the window.

His expression turned serious as he set his cup in the saucer and met her gaze. "I saw Sandra Westport yesterday."

"Oh?"

"I understand now why you said you were the last person she'd want to have lunch with."

"Oh," she said.

"Yeah. I know about the offer she and David made you. Being the public face for their project is a good opportunity."

"Not for someone who has no face to offer," she countered.

"What about offering hope to kids going through all kinds of stuff kids shouldn't have to go through?" He looked completely sincere. "It's a really worthwhile undertaking."

"I never said it wasn't meaningful," she insisted.

"If anything, what you've been through, the accident and everything since, would give you more credibility as a spokeswoman. Who would know better than someone who's been to hell and back that this camp would give kids something to look forward to?"

His words struck a chord within her. She would always remember the pain and despair. But the worst of the ordeal had been a future without light. She tipped her head as she looked at him. "Has anyone ever told you you've got a way with words? If I'm ever in trouble with the law, I want you."

He had the strangest look on his face—part longing, part regret. Then he smiled and the expression disappeared. "You're too good to ever be in trouble. But if you ever need me, I'm there."

She sighed. "I appreciate a different perspective, but I keep going back to the fact that they haven't seen my face for themselves. They may not want me."

"Not a chance. You are and always will be an exceptionally beautiful woman." The gleam in his eyes added the weight of sincerity to his words.

But she still didn't believe. "I appreciate the lie. But I've learned to only see the positive when I look in the mirror."

He reached over and took her hand in his own. "When you look in the mirror, if you don't like what you see, just look in my eyes."

Her breath caught at the words and the intensely honest expression on his handsome face. Hope flitted at the edges of her mind but she refused to embrace it.

She pulled her hand away from his. "They say beauty is only skin deep and no one realizes better than me how true that is. My career was a selfish, shallow, superficial pursuit."

"I don't think the people you helped to sell millions of dollars worth of cosmetics and hair products would agree with you," he said wryly.

She shrugged. "It wasn't a very noble profession.

And it still begs the question—why did the professor send for me?"

"I can't answer that. But I submit that if the missed opportunities really bother you, being involved with this kids' camp is your chance to make a difference."

Helpless to refute his words, she simply shook her head. "You're a very persuasive man."

"It's an acquired skill," he said modestly.

"Well, you're very skilled at it. I'll think about what you said."

"Fair enough."

But it wasn't at all fair when he smiled his devastatingly attractive smile, and her gaze was instantly drawn to his mouth. Her heart skipped a beat as she wondered what it would feel like against her own. She'd been too upset to remember. After all these years, she felt as if she could let down her guard with Nate and sink into his arms—and be safe.

The sad thing was that the way she'd acted, he would probably be afraid to ever touch her intimately again. And oh, how she wanted him to. She desperately wanted a do-over with him. But the poor man had called from outside her room to warn her he was going to knock. How pathetic was that? Even worse were the thoughts of him that continuously popped into her mind.

She didn't know how to stop it.

The worst part was: she didn't know if she wanted to.

She looked at him and realized she was becoming accustomed to the fluttering in her chest. "For the record, next time you're tempted to call me from your cell phone in the hall outside my room?"

"Yes?"

"Just knock on the connecting door," she invited.

His grin turned the fluttering up a notch, maybe two. But not to worry. It wouldn't be long until they could meet with the college board of directors on behalf of the professor, then she and Nate would part ways for good.

Nate tossed the paperwork for Ted Hawkins's appeal onto the coffee table. It seemed profane to be working on this with Katie in the room next door. He didn't know what the guy had done to her, but it wasn't good. That wasn't woo-woo supernatural talking, just connecting the dots. Ten years ago she'd been more upset than a breakup with her college boyfriend warranted and researching Ted's current legal quagmire had uncovered a pattern of questionable behavior in regard to sexual assault. It was amazing no one had brought charges before now. But Nate wished he'd never taken the case and seeing Katie again hadn't generated the feelings. He'd felt that way as soon as the slime king had walked into his office.

Sighing, Nate walked over to the window and looked outside. Dusk had just settled and dim lights marched up the street. Thoughts of Katie had him wanting very much to see her, be with her. He started to pull his cell from the holster on his belt then remembered what she'd said about knocking on the connecting door between their rooms. He hoped she wasn't simply being polite, but was beginning to trust him. He knocked softly and waited.

The bolt on her side clicked just before the door opened. "Hi."

She was wearing the same white cotton blouse that clung to her small, firm breasts and the same worn jeans that hugged her gently curved hips and long slender legs. She'd looked exceedingly cute this morning and his heart-pounding reaction now only proved that absence makes the heart grow fonder.

"Hi yourself." He leaned against the desk beside the door and folded his arms over his chest, tucking his shaking hands into his armpits. "Are you busy?"

She shrugged. "Not unless you call watching *Star Trek* reruns hectic and demanding. What about you?"

His chest squeezed tight when he remembered what he'd been doing and he glanced over his shoulder. The folder was facedown. "Paperwork."

"Sounds exciting."

"You have no idea." And if he was lucky, she never would. "Since I don't have scheduled court appearances, I can work from here and stay in touch with the office by phone. But I'm ready for a break. Want to blow this popsicle stand? Just a walk for some fresh air?"

Her smile was reluctant. "We went through this at breakfast."

"The sun is down," he pointed out, cocking his thumb toward the window.

"I don't know—"

"It's too dark for anyone to see you, let alone recognize you. But here's the deal. If there's a rogue paparazzo out there waiting to pounce, I swear I'll protect you."

Laughter crinkled the corners of her eyes and for just an instant, the lightness and genuine amusement seemed to make her scars disappear. "You win, counselor."

Usually, but not in Ted's case. He shook his head, pushing away the dark thoughts. He'd made Katie laugh and if he could, he'd do it again.

As they left the Paul Revere Inn, Nate made a great show of shielding her and slipping into clandestine mode, peeking around corners before venturing out. By the time they were on Saunders University turf, he could tell Katie had relaxed. As they leisurely strolled the grounds, a light warm summer breeze washed over him along with the memories. He recalled the fountain Katie must have loved because he knew he could always find her there. Sometimes he'd keep out of sight and simply look at her. Other times he worked up the nerve to say hello. Always she was friendly and kind.

He pointed to the fountain, the white frothy water gently illuminated by spotlights strategically placed in the cobblestone square. "Remember that?"

"Oh, my. I used to come here all the time. To think. The gurgling water made me feel peaceful. Usually," she said, a dark tone creeping into her voice.

"I used to come here, too." He refused to tell her why. No point in giving her a frame of reference to remember him.

She looked up and studied him intently, then shook her head. "I wish I could remember you. I'm sorry."

Not him. He was glad she had a memory lapse. "Trust me, you're not missing anything."

She stuck her hands in the pockets of her jeans. "You're a very good lawyer, Nate Williams."

Oh, God. Instantly, he glanced at her but the night shadows hid her expression. She didn't remember him from college, but maybe she knew he'd been lead chair for some of the most infamous, headlines-grabbing cases in recent memory.

"Why do you say that?" Classic avoidance technique.

"Because I've been on the receiving end of your cross-examination numerous times since we ran into each other."

"Literally."

"Yes," she agreed. "And you've grilled practically my whole life out of me. But I know almost nothing about you."

Her voice was light and teasing, without a hint of accusation. Meaning his secret was still safe. He blew out a long breath. "I guess that's because there's not much to tell. I'm just not a very interesting guy."

"I think you're wrong."

Hot damn and hallelujah, he thought. Shrugging he said, "I'm just a hardworking attorney."

"It must be so gratifying to have the power to help people."

He wasn't going to tell her it was all about smoke and mirrors to produce reasonable doubt in jurors' minds. But he hadn't set out to be famous. He'd only wanted to make a good living and this is what he'd turned into. He never wanted her to know he was a master of spin. He never wanted her to doubt his sincerity about her. She was good and kind and it was so very wrong that a drunk driver had scarred her forever.

"Speaking of helping people," he said, "Did you ever receive a settlement from your accident?"

Her laugh was bitter. "Hardly. The guy had nothing. No license, no insurance, no job. All he had was a blood alcohol level twice the legal limit. I had to pay for what my medical insurance didn't cover and it wiped me out financially."

His gut tightened with anger. That really put into perspective the scope of her injuries. His hands clenched as he wished for five minutes alone with the drunk who'd done this to her.

"I didn't mean to tell you that. I'm sorry."

"I'm not." He looked at her. "Is there anything I can do to help?"

She shook her head. "Actually, I'm glad you know. I want to help the professor. But I can't afford to stay here indefinitely."

His chest tightened with regret and guilt. She was the kind of person he'd intended to help when he'd made up his mind to study law. "I could probably get you something."

She looked up and in the dim light her eyes were sad. "You can't get me back what I need most. My face. My life."

"Then you need a new life."

"Is that so?" Her tone was wry. "Just like that?"

"People reinvent themselves all the time." He grinned. "Look at Madonna."

"Trust me when I say no one wants to hear me sing." She sighed. "No. My face was my fortune."

Damn her parents for hammering that into her, for limiting her. "That's bull. You're an intelligent woman.

The professor knew it ten years ago and I know it now."

"I believe you believe that. But it doesn't answer the big question. What am I going to be when I grow up?"

"Anything you want."

As they walked in the shadows, their hands brushed. Nate reached over and linked his fingers with hers. He held his breath, waiting to see if she'd pull away. She didn't, and to his amazement, she squeezed his hand and swayed against him, putting her other hand on his arm.

"I'd forgotten how romantic this campus is," she commented.

"Maybe it wasn't when we were here."

"No. It hasn't changed. It still feels romantic."

Was she trying to tell him something? His heart jumped and his blood pumped hot and fast through his veins. He looked down at her, and when she looked back, he wished he could read her mind. He wanted to kiss her more than anything, but he didn't want to scare her again. In every way he knew how, he'd tried to show her he wouldn't hurt her. They said third time's the charm. But if he was reading her wrong, there would be no third time to charm her.

She had the sweetest body he'd ever seen and his fingers ached to know every hollow and curve. But her "romantic" remark could be as explosive as a truck filled with C4. He had no idea what she was telling him. So much for the hotshot attorney who prided himself on his ability to read people's body language. For all the information he was getting from her, she might as well be speaking in Swahili.

"Tell you what," he said. "Tomorrow I'll try to see Alex Broadstreet again."

"Who's he?"

"The Chairman of the college board of directors. I'll see if I'm a good enough attorney to shake things up and get the process moving faster."

"Thank you, Nate."

They were near enough to a light on the path for him to see her shimmering sweet smile. It looked welcoming, but what if she was simply grateful? He couldn't afford to take a chance.

Unless his radar gave him clear signals, he would continue to play Boy Scout, knight in shining armor, or anything else she wanted for as long as she would let him.

Or as long as his secrets stayed secret.

Chapter Seven

It was early afternoon when Nate pulled into the hotel parking lot and turned off the car's ignition. If only he could shut off his anger and frustration as easily, but the only key was meeting face-to-face with Alex Broadstreet. And the man was still dodging him.

He walked toward the hotel and as he passed an open area, something red and fluttery caught his eye. Someone was sitting in the gazebo, he noticed. His skin felt hot and his heart pounded and he knew it was Katie. She was almost completely concealed by the lush ivy intertwining with the white lattice, but somehow he'd known she was there. Some sort of invisible Katie-radar.

He changed course and stepped up into the semienclosed structure. She tensed until she recognized him and the relief that jumped into her expression meant she trusted him. He was glad.

"What happened with Alex Broadstreet?" she asked, adjusting the red silk scarf covering her hair and the left side of her face.

He sat beside her, close enough that his thigh brushed hers. The slight contact created sparks that instantly heated his blood and he was surprised that it took so little to do that.

But this wasn't about him or her. "I didn't see Broadstreet."

"What?" Her hand hovered over her mouth.

"He refused to see me."

"Do you know why?"

"I didn't have an appointment."

"And?"

"How did you know there was more?" he asked.

"I could just tell."

He'd like to think she had some sort of radar where he was concerned. That thought almost lifted his mood. But almost was only important in horseshoes and hand grenades. He knew how important it was for her to help the professor and if she was going to be able to, something had to break soon. Therein was the source of his frustration. He'd felt as if he'd failed her.

"I made the mistake of telling his secretary why I was there." He held back his suspicion that Broadstreet knew him by name and go-for-the-jugular reputation. By some miracle, Katie had had no idea he was infamous and he wanted to keep his flaws secret for as long as possible.

"So Professor Harrison's name was the kiss of death?" she asked.

He nodded. "Almost literally. I threatened to barge into Broadstreet's office and she grabbed the phone to call security."

"Oh, Nate." Disappointment hovered in her eyes. "Now what are we going to do?"

"It wasn't a total loss."

"You got an appointment," she guessed.

"Yeah." He ran his fingers through his hair. "In ten days."

"Ten days!" She stood and spread her hands wide, a helpless, frustrated gesture. "Why so long?"

"That's what I wanted to know. Unfortunately, no one would give me any answers." He rested his elbows on his knees and linked his fingers together. "So I guess I'm not such a good lawyer after all."

She sat down and rested her small palm on his forearm. "I'm sure that's not true. Even the best attorney can't get results when someone is uncooperative and deliberately delaying matters. You need to cut yourself some slack."

"I'm not used to doing that." His arm tingled from the warmth of her fingers and he struggled to ignore the sensation and concentrate on her worried expression. "And the question is what do we do now?"

"There's no question. We have to wait him out. And that's a problem for me," she said, linking her fingers together in her lap.

"What are you going to do?" He held his breath.

"I know what I can't do." She pinched off an ivy leaf and twirled it. "I can't afford to stay here in the hotel and there's no way I can fly back and forth from California when smarmy Mr. Broadstreet decides to see us."

"I could help. The hotel bill—"

"I won't take money from you."

"It's not a hardship, Katie. I can afford it."

"No." She shook her head, then tossed the leaf aside.

"I want to do something for you. For him. He may need all of us. Who knows what might sway the board in the professor's favor?"

"Okay. You're right." She thought for several moments. "But there's more than one way to get my message across."

He was pretty sure he wasn't going to like this. "What are you thinking?"

"Maybe I could put my testimonial in writing."

"I don't know—"

"I could do it from home. And you're an attorney. I could e-mail it to you to look over and make sure it's persuasive, then send it to the board. Hopefully, along with good words from more of his students it will be enough to convince them to keep him on staff."

Nate shook his head. That meant she'd leave. It was a terrible plan, even though he knew that if she stayed, sooner or later he would have to confess who he used to be and what he was now. Everything in him cried out against that, too. It tore him apart to think about her disappointment and revulsion if she knew he was that unappealing geek. Or the slick lawyer who worked on behalf of criminal defendants. But even worse was the idea of letting her go when he'd only just found her again.

There must be another way. For God's sake, he could persuade juries to do whatever he wanted. Surely he could convince her not to go. All he had to do was put his heart into it.

He looked at her. The afternoon sunlight filtered through the vines and caressed her face, making her soft skin luminous. She would always be the most beautiful woman he'd ever seen.

"I'd be happy to help you put your thoughts into words," he offered. "But a face-to-face tribute would be far more persuasive, especially when the face is as lovely as yours."

Her full lips turned up at the corners. "Liar."

If she only knew, he thought.

"It's the God's honest truth," he said.

"You really believe that delivering my acknowledgment in person would be better?"

"Yes. And I'm being completely honest when I say that you always were and still are an incredibly beautiful woman."

She smiled at him. In the few days they'd been together, she'd changed from the solitary, withdrawn, wounded woman he'd first encountered. She'd put aside her personal problems for the sake of a friend and was gaining strength in the process. The wary expression was fading from her eyes and she looked at him with more confidence every day. He didn't want to hinder that progress or slow it down. And he was afraid that's exactly what would happen if she went back to California.

So, she needed to stay. And he could help her.

"Look," he said. "I've got a crazy idea."

"Crazy?" she said, arching one dark eyebrow. "Not a good way to start, counselor."

"Okay. I have a brilliant suggestion."

"Better. I'm listening."

He blew out a breath. In court he'd stand and face the jury, make eye contact and be as intimidating as possible. He wouldn't do that with her. Except for the eye contact. And he would be as sincere as possible. That was the easy part. But this was too important to make a wrong move. "I live about two hours from the college. A condo on the other side of Boston."

"Okay."

"It's a big place. Way more room than I need."

"Uh-huh."

He studied her face, waiting for the guarded expression. When he didn't see it, he continued. "There's plenty of room for a guest."

"Oh?"

"In fact, the extra room is as far from the master bedroom as one can get and still be in the same county." When she laughed, he knew the words had exactly the effect he'd hoped for. "You're welcome to stay with me."

The humor faded as she caught her bottom lip between her teeth. "I don't know, Nate."

"I do. It would be nice for a bachelor like myself to have the company. People are starting to talk about the eccentric guy who lives all alone and talks to himself."

"Oh, please."

"I'm serious." He grinned. "Almost."

"You're positive I wouldn't be in the way?"

"Absolutely. It's only ten days. Not that long." Then a thought struck him. "Unless you've got commitments."

She laughed with the barest hint of bitterness. "One needs a life before one can have commitments. I don't have one, remember?"

"When I said that—"

"It's all right." She put up a hand. "I know how you meant it."

"So, will you do me and the professor a favor and stay here until the meeting with Alex Broadstreet? What do you say?"

She blew out a long breath as she thought for several moments. Then she met his gaze and smiled. "I say thanks. I'd be happy to accept your kind invitation."

"Excellent," he said.

It was hard not to grab her in his arms and kiss her. Exhilaration coursed through him and suddenly he wondered when, if ever, he'd been this happy.

"I hope you won't be sorry." She smiled her lovely sweet smile and he felt it all the way to his soul.

In that instant he realized his invitation was dangerous. And tenuous. And fragile. But he took chances every time he accepted a client, walked into a courtroom or delivered a summation to a jury. The only difference—that was always about someone else's life and future. This was his. But it was done now and the truth was he wouldn't take it back even if he could. No matter what happened to him, he couldn't turn his back on her.

She stood. "I'll try to be as inconspicuous as possible. You won't even know I'm there."

She couldn't be more wrong; his Katie-radar was functioning perfectly. "I'm sure you'll be a perfect houseguest."

"I can do that. It's only ten days."

Maybe only ten days to her. To him it could be a lifetime.

It was weak and spineless and probably offensive to every feminist on the planet, but Kathryn couldn't help feeling pampered and protected as Nate muscled her luggage out of his car and into the elevator taking them to his condo on the building's top floor. He'd handled it at the hotel, too, and a lot more. When it was time to leave, he'd come to her room and casually mentioned he'd already checked her out. Oddly enough, he didn't have a receipt with the list of charges on her credit card. And she'd been under the impression that lawyers were detail oriented. Since he wouldn't respond to her direct questions, she had a strong feeling he'd taken care of her bill.

"You know I'm going to pay you back," she said as the elevator raced smoothly upward.

He looked at her, the three-dimensional picture of innocence. "Is that a threat?"

"Of course not. It's a promise." She laughed. "I have a sneaking suspicion you paid my hotel bill."

"I plead the fifth."

"There's nothing incriminating about being a nice guy," she said.

"From your mouth to God's ear," he answered, again looking so innocent she had to laugh.

"I didn't say you were a Boy Scout," she teased.

"Good thing. You'd be wrong."

"How can you say that?" She stared at him, but the elevator doors whispered open before he could respond.

"Straight ahead," he said, indicating the double doors in front of them.

His place. She waited for the knot to form in her stomach, but nothing happened. Of course she couldn't believe how easily he'd talked her into being his "roomie." Partly she was grateful to put off for just a little longer going home and "getting a life." But mostly she wanted a little more time with Nate. Plain and simple, she liked being with him. He was funny and sweet and made her feel safe. Too safe, maybe.

The other night when they'd walked memory lane at Saunders, he'd taken her hand. And she hadn't flinched away. In fact, she'd grown so comfortable, she'd brushed against him, touched his arm and generally tried to let him know she wouldn't mind if he kissed her again. But he never tried.

Using his key, he opened the door and let her precede him into the circular foyer of his place. The area was a rotunda with a high, inset ceiling and canned lighting. Straight ahead she noticed a two-way fireplace with a gas log enclosed by glass doors. On the other side it opened on the living room. To her right was a room and a quick glance at the bookshelves, desk and computer identified it as an office.

"This is beautiful," she said.

"Thanks." He looked around, an expression of pride on his face.

"I mean, this is really nice. Bland word. The professor would be disappointed." She glanced around, trying to take it all in. "I've seen a lot of places in Beverly Hills, Bel Air, Malibu. I've been to launch parties for cosmetics companies in some ultra hoity-toity places.

This is right up there. You must be a really good lawyer."

He looked decidedly uncomfortable. "How about I show you where you're going to bunk?"

"Okay."

He led her into the kitchen–family room combination. "That way is the master bedroom," he said, pointing down the hall. "This way is the guest wing."

"A whole wing for little old me?"

He shrugged. "What can I say? I'm a gracious host."

And then some, she thought. He was making it a point to show her that his room was on the other side of the place. Just as he'd told her. What he didn't know was that if she hadn't believed him then, she wouldn't have accepted his invitation at all.

And now, she really wanted another chance to kiss him. He was sweet and kind, but he was also one of the best-looking men she'd ever seen. He made her heart race in a way it hadn't for longer than she could remember. When he was near, there was a catch in her breathing and her limbs went weak. But she'd pushed him away when he'd kissed her. How in the world would he know she was wildly attracted? And telling him so could be too humiliating. So, apparently, they were destined for a lovely friendship. If she were a glass-is-half-full kind of person, letting a man back into her life even as a friend was a step in the right direction. But the woman inside her was coming back to life. And that woman wanted more than friendship.

Nate carried her suitcase and toiletries bag down the hall and she admired his broad back, sighing with vague regret when he turned right into the bedroom. She smiled with delight when she looked around.

"This is completely charming," she said.

A Laura Ashley floral print comforter covered the queen-size bed along with coordinating bed skirt, sheets and ruffled shams. The brass headboard gave it an old-fashioned, homey feel. On each elegant cherry-wood nightstand rested a Waterford lamp with a cream-colored brocade shade decorated with hanging crystals. A matching dresser and armoire sat on opposite walls and a variety of oval-framed needlepoint pictures mixed with pastel watercolor paintings finished off the decorating.

"So you like it?" He set her luggage down on the antique cedar chest at the foot of the bed.

She met his gaze. "Who wouldn't? But I have to say it's a surprise."

"Why?" There was the barest hint of sharpness in the single word.

"It doesn't seem like your style."

"Should I take that as a compliment?"

"Since it's quite a feminine room and you're a pretty macho guy, I'd say definitely a compliment."

"Would it help if I said I had a decorator?"

"And did you give her carte blanche? Or did you direct her to make it girly for the women in your life?"

The idea of other women stopped her in her tracks. Something stung in the center of her chest and she realized, to her surprise, that it was jealousy. For so long she hadn't cared about a man, let alone about rivals for his affection. She'd always just been pathetically grateful when men hit on anyone besides her. But Nate was different and he brought out unfamiliar feelings in her.

He studied the room. "I just told her to do what she liked. I confess I hardly use this part of the place."

"She has good taste. Is she pretty?"

His forehead puckered as he frowned. "I don't remember."

That made her happy. "I'd like the rest of the tour."

"Your wish is my command." He held out his hand. "This room has a private bath."

She peeked in. There were double sinks with gold fixtures and a separate tub and shower. The walk-in closet was big. In essence, this was another master suite. He showed her the other three bedrooms. Two had the same traditional touches and the last was a well-used home gym. He obviously worked at keeping his impressive physique…impressive. When he led her back to the family room, she realized he'd deliberately omitted his bedroom from the tour. Another gesture to make her comfortable. She couldn't decide whether it was working or simply frustrating her.

In the family room, the chenille-covered side-by-side recliners were tucked into the corner in front of an expensive-looking big-screen TV. She hadn't been so completely out of it for the last year that she didn't know affluence when she saw it—even of the technical variety. He'd said he was well off; he hadn't lied.

And she was beginning to expect nothing less of Nate. But what had surprised her was the intriguing combination of traditional comfort mixed in with the obviously expensive and luxurious furnishings. He was a reflection of his surroundings—a uniquely complex man.

In the entertainment alcove she noticed built-in shelves beside the TV and more canned lighting. Curios and knickknacks were scattered around, but an elegant platinum frame caught her eye. She picked up the photo to study the sweet-faced older woman. "Who's this?"

He took it from her and a tender expression crept into his eyes. "My grandmother."

"She looks like a lovely woman."

"She was." A note of sadness mixed with regret softened his voice.

"I never knew my grandparents," she said.

"I hardly knew my parents." He put the photo back and met her gaze. "Are you hungry?"

Wow, way to abruptly change the subject, she thought.

"I'm starved," she admitted, realizing she'd been too preoccupied with his digs to notice. "But first I have a question."

"Shoot," he said, looking as though he literally expected her to pull out an assault rifle and blast away.

She studied the keepsakes strewn about. "Are there any pictures of you? I mean from high school? Or college. Something that would trigger a memory for me." It was a rhetorical question, because the photo of his grandmother was the only personal memento she could see.

He shook his head. "I don't have any pictures."

"None?"

"Nope."

She knew he was a guy. And in general guys weren't as sentimental about that sort of thing. But still... None?

"I still don't have a clear memory of you," she said, shaking her head.

He nodded. "Good."

"Why do you say that?"

"It's not a time I like to remember."

"But, Nate, surely you have a photo tucked away—"

"I've got a nice bottle of Cabernet." He took her elbow and steered her into the kitchen. For a clever and outgoing man he'd given her a not-so-subtle clue that he didn't want to talk about his past. Why?

"Let's open the wine and I'll order in Italian." He picked up the phone and dialed.

"You know the number by heart?"

"I don't cook much."

Did women cook for him? Again the green-eyed monster tweaked her as she pictured him having wine and pasta with his interior decorator who'd done such a lovely job on the guest suite. Kathryn reminded herself she had no claim on him. She'd lost the right when he kissed her and she'd pushed him away. It was too bad she'd blown her chance, because way down deep inside she was getting a feeling that she could have something with Nate.

But she wanted to remember the man who remembered her and to find out why he had no reminders of that time. She wanted to know more about the man he was now. And that was one more reason she was glad she'd accepted his invitation.

In spite of the fact that he'd paid someone to decorate, surely she could find hints of the real Nate Williams here in his personal space.

Chapter Eight

Kathryn took a sip from her second glass of wine and savored the warmth that coursed through her. Or maybe it was the buzz. Either way she felt pretty relaxed as she studied Nate across from her. She loved this kitchen with the earth-tone granite countertops and solid birch cupboards. The table wasn't new, in fact it looked like an antique. In really excellent shape. The dark wood was shined to perfection and a matching buffet with inlaid wood was tucked underneath the window.

"That was probably the best ravioli in tomato cream sauce I've ever had," she said.

"Can I cook, or what?"

"You dial a phone better than anyone I've ever seen," she countered.

"Why, I believe that's the nicest thing you've ever said to me." His grin made her warmer than the wine.

"Who are you, Nate Williams?"

"What do you mean?"

The instant frown was such a contrast to his smile, she was startled. "I just can't help wondering about you. For instance, this place."

"What about it?"

She glanced around. "I'd have figured you for the type who would display expensive art, along with the proper lighting."

The dark look lifted, replaced by his trademark grin. "Are you calling me a snob?"

"If snobs collect paintings with two heads, mismatched eyes and arms so out of proportion they would drag the curb on a real person, then yes. That would be my impression of you."

He laughed. "I'm not a big fan of that style. Give me an ocean or water scene any day."

"Me, too," she agreed. "But seriously, I can't reconcile the man who would have oval-framed needlepoint and this beautiful old table with the person who would live in this pricey high-rise on the top floor."

"Top is the best."

"Is that important to you? Being the best?"

"It's more about success. But I guess that's just semantics. Winners have to be the best."

"So in your top floor condo, you've got needlepoint on the walls and a table from a different era. What's that about?"

He shrugged. "They belonged to my grandmother."

"So family is important, too?"

"Of course. You sound surprised that I have family."

"I just didn't think about you with family."

"I wasn't raised by wolves."

"I was," she said.

"That's harsh." He grinned, chasing the shadows from his face.

"I suppose. And probably my folks were just being practical in their outlook. When you've got a tight budget, I suppose their attitude makes sense. And I never went without what I really needed because my mom put me in a lot of those little girl's beauty pageants. I placed or won a lot and the prize money helped stretch the budget. But it would have made more sense to encourage an education with possibilities instead of putting all my eggs in one basket." She met his gaze, grateful there was no pity in it. "When that basket is taken away, it's free fall."

"I don't think your basket is kaput."

His comment surprised her. "How can you say that?"

"You made a name for yourself, Katie. And you've got a lot to offer."

"I don't see it."

"You will," he promised.

"I think the altitude up here in your pricey place is making you light-headed."

"Not the altitude." His eyes took on a gleam that made her heart pound. "The lovely company."

She drained the last of her wine. "I've been meaning to ask. Have you had your eyesight checked recently?"

"Yes, as a matter of fact. I just got new contacts."

"Really?"

"You sound surprised."

"I am. You just seem so…perfect."

"Trust me. I'm not. Not even close."

She studied the tightness around his mouth and realized she was no closer to discovering the real Nate Williams than she had been when she'd walked into his space. Then a yawn slipped out and she covered it with her hand.

"Sorry," she said. "I guess I'm more tired than I realized." She stood up. "I'll help you clean up."

"No. I'll take care of it. You get some rest."

She nodded. "See you in the morning."

"Sleep well."

Maybe. But she had a feeling with him so close she was going to have more of a princess-and-the-pea night.

Nate looked up from his book after he'd read the same page for the umpteenth time and still didn't know what it said. His mind was too full of Katie. Clearly she was curious about him and his surroundings had triggered questions. Bringing her here had probably been a big mistake. But the alternative would have been to let her go and that was unacceptable. However he looked at it, he'd been between a rock and a hard place. And if Katie was there with him, it wasn't a bad place to be.

She'd pleaded weariness and gone to bed an hour or so before, but he hadn't been able to sleep. He looked around his bedroom with the masculine oak furniture and geometric design comforter and felt the loneliness pressing in on him. He'd always been a loner and thought he'd come to terms with it. Why did he feel more isolated and alone with her under his roof? He sighed. Because she was so near and yet so far. Because the more he was around her, the harder it was to not touch her, to not kiss her the way he wanted. And he wouldn't cross that line. He would never hurt her.

He had faced the fact that she was and would always only be his friend.

He thought he heard a noise. Or was it just an excuse to look in on her? When his ten days more with her were up, he wouldn't be able to walk a few feet down the hall to make sure she was all right. Was she having another nightmare? In every way possible he'd tried to make her feel safe, but the change of scene and being in an unfamiliar place might have resurrected her bad memories. He put the book down and went to see if she needed him.

When he saw the door to the guest room open, he peeked in and found her gone. His heart pounded as he went to check the front door and saw a light on in his office off the entryway. Maybe she hadn't been able to sleep, either, and had gone to find a book. He'd told her to make herself at home.

Without a word, he stood in the doorway. She was there in her short pink terry cloth robe. Just below the hem he saw a long scar from the surgery to repair her shattered leg. Outrage and fury surged through him and he grabbed onto them to keep from feeling other more dangerous and painful emotions.

When the red haze cleared enough, he realized what

she was holding—his college yearbook. With a sinking feeling, he realized what she was looking at. Why the hell had he kept it all these years? Then he remembered. There were pictures of Katie—cheerleader, homecoming queen, girl most likely to never know he was alive. For a man who prided himself on thinking things through, clearly Nate had dropped the ball when he'd invited her to stay here.

Quietly he walked into the room. She gasped in surprise when he gently took the yearbook from her fingers. "Nate! Good Lord, you scared me."

He closed the book. "I forgot about this when I said I didn't have any pictures."

"I couldn't sleep and was looking for a book. I'm sorry if I invaded your personal space." She studied him. "But I remember you now. They called you—"

"Wide Load Willie or whatever clever name they could come up with. Alliteration was not my friend in those days." He tried to keep the bitterness out of his voice, but knew he was only marginally successful.

"They teased you unmercifully." She moved in front of him and met his gaze, her own swimming with sympathy. "I can only imagine how painful it was for you."

"They say playing sports builds character. For me, teasing was a competitive sport."

"I suppose it's no consolation, but you have more character than any man I've ever met. Why didn't you tell me who you really are?"

When she reached up a hand to touch his face, he knew she remembered the scars that used to be there. He instinctively ducked away, then turned to put the book back on the bottom shelf.

"I didn't say anything because I left that guy behind. I didn't want you to remember the brainer geek I was. And geek is a step up. Freak rhymes with geek and they used to have some fun with that."

"Didn't the professor used to say that unintelligent people called others names and swore like marines because they were too dim and dense to have a decent vocabulary?"

"Yeah." Now he understood, but at the time it hadn't helped a whole lot. "Anyway, it's over."

"If you say so, but it's still a part of you. It's why you understood how I felt." She moved forward again and this time he stood his ground when she reached up and cupped his cheek with her small hand. "You certainly look different."

"It's amazing the things money can buy."

"What does that mean?" She frowned and pulled her hand back.

"When I was a starving student, I could barely afford an education. That's not whining. It's just the facts. When I finally passed the bar and became an attorney, I had more money than I'd ever seen in my life." He shrugged. "So I hired a personal trainer and went to a plastic surgeon."

"He did a good job." She traced the scar below her eye. "In my case all they could do was minimize the damage. It was explained to me that every time an incision was made, it was invasive. They could take the tiniest stitches with the finest possible suturing material, but there would still be a scar. And the greater the trauma, the less they can do. Doctors play God every day and we expect miracles. But there are limitations."

"I found out the only limitations are the ones we put on ourselves." He stared into her eyes. "In spite of the way I looked, I was determined to make something of myself."

"And you did," she said, glancing around his oak-paneled office with the leather furniture. "People depend on you."

Her expression was so earnest, so trusting. If she only knew, money couldn't buy everything. It had bought him confidence, but cost him self-respect. Now that one of his secrets was out, would the others fall like dominoes? Would it cost him even more?

She sighed and lowered her gaze. "No one is depending on me, Nate. No one counts on me."

"Not true." He pulled his hands from his pockets in an instinctive need to hold her, and touch her. Then he curled his fingers into his palms. If he touched her, he wasn't sure he had the willpower to keep from kissing her. And if he kissed her, he was going to do more.

"I count on you," he said simply. "In college you were always there with a kind word, a smile. That's what got me through."

"I had no idea." Then her eyes widened. "It's like now that I know, the floodgates are open. How could I forget?"

"What?" he asked sharply.

There was a distant expression on her face and she winced, as if remembering some long-ago pain. "I get it now. I understand why from the first moment I saw you again your voice was so reassuring. It was you—"

"What?" he asked again.

"That night. I—I was upset when I left the fraternity house. I—I had broken up w-with Ted." She linked her fingers, rubbed her hands together nervously, then turned away. "You were there. You comforted me."

He'd held her in his arms while she cried, and been angrier with Ted Hawkins than he'd ever been in his life. "I remember. But all I did was listen."

"No. You talked to me. I don't even remember what you said, but the way you said it. In that wonderful soft deep voice. It was so reassuring. I responded to it then and again at the hotel. Even when I didn't remember who you were, I knew that voice all these years later."

"I'm glad I could help."

Although she'd spent all these years trying to forget, Kathryn remembered that night. Ted hadn't taken no for an answer. Not about her breaking it off and not when she'd refused to sleep with him. He hurt and humiliated her. But Nate had held her in his arms until she pulled herself together.

So many memories came flooding back now that she knew his true identity. She stared at him. "Helped? That's an understatement. Even after that, as I recall, we were pretty good friends until you left for law school."

"Yeah."

"You didn't stay in touch. Why?"

"Busy." He shrugged. "I had to study hard to keep my grades up. Had to be the best."

"Because of?"

"I guess I was finally in a place where ability was recognized. It gave me confidence. And you know the rest."

Did she? she wondered, recognizing shadows on his face. But that could wait. She'd found him again. He'd been there for her that night and she'd not let any other man close since. She moved in front of him, a whisper away, and saw the intensity in his gaze. She was pretty sure he wanted her.

"So you found the confidence to live your life?" she questioned.

"Yeah."

She reached up and put her arms around his neck. "Show me what I have to live for," she pleaded.

His gaze caught fire, but he said, "Katie, no. You don't know what you're asking."

"I do."

"You'll hate yourself in the morning," he warned. "You'll hate me."

"Never." She shook her head.

Ever since that horrible night she'd been trying to bury the painful memories of the assault. She'd been violated in a way no woman should be. Finally, after all this time and against all the odds, she'd found this man again. Even more miraculous, she wanted him to make love to her. She needed to replace that nightmare with a beautiful memory. Nate was the right man and this was the right time. She needed this life-affirming act to begin healing.

Please God, she wouldn't freeze up again—or worse—push him away. Because Nate had been hurt, too. And she wouldn't hurt him again. Not for the world.

"Please, Nate—"

"Katie, I— Are you sure?" When she nodded, he tightened his hold, pulling her against him.

She laughed nervously, but the sound held no humor. "I know you said guys dig chicks with scars, but—I'm not like I was in college."

"Neither am I." Gently he cupped her face in his palms, then kissed her left cheek and the scar there. "I want you, Katie. I've always wanted you. For as long as I can remember. But I need to know. Are you sure this is what you really want?"

She nodded. "I've never been more sure of anything in my life."

"Thank God." He let out a long shuddering breath and his eyes took on an intensity that thrilled her. "Because I don't have the strength to refuse you anything."

And then he touched his mouth to hers. Gently. He kissed her as if it was his very first time—soft, sweet, tentative, exploring.

When he pulled back, he stared into her eyes, searching for permission, for approval, for proof that she was okay.

"How'd you get to be such a good kisser?" she asked.

"You taught me. Just now."

She smiled. "Nate, you left your bedroom off the tour. Will you show it to me now?"

He nodded. "You're calling the shots. Your wish is my command."

Chapter Nine

Kathryn linked her fingers with Nate's and let him lead her through the family room and down the hall to the left—toward his bedroom. She tensed and instantly he looked at her, assessing, as if he were completely attuned to every cell, nerve and muscle in her body.

"Are you sure about this, Katie? If you're not—"

She shook her head. "I'm sure."

If he knew she wasn't absolutely certain, he'd back off. She believed that with every fiber of her being. This was Nate, gentle and understanding. He had no idea why she'd been so upset that night, but he'd stayed with her and emotionally nursed her through the worst night of her life. Seeing him again had helped her regain a sense of safety which made this right. That and the warm wonderful feeling inside when he'd kissed her. Instead of disappearing, her response had grown more intense. The way her heart was pounding gave her hope that this could be the best night—the first night of the rest of her life.

In the hall, he stopped at the threshold of the master bedroom's double-door entry and looked down at her. "This is it."

She walked inside and glanced around, getting a vague impression of large, masculine, matching oak furniture. The bed was king-size, but that made sense for a man as tall as Nate. The comforter and blanket had been turned down, exposing the bottom sheet. He was still dressed in jeans and shirt, but she wondered if he'd been preparing for bed. Her gaze darted beyond it, to the sitting area with two wing chairs and a brass table lamp between them holding a book facedown.

More than a little nervous, she moved past the bed, maybe putting things off just a little longer. She picked up his book and saw that her hand was shaking. "The latest techno thriller."

Still standing in the doorway, he lifted one broad shoulder. "It's relaxing."

"I suppose losing yourself in fiction is one way of relieving stress. I imagine you're under a lot of pressure."

"You could say that."

Her gaze jumped to his and she saw the barest hint of a smile flirting with the corners of his mouth. But his eyes never lost their intensity and she knew what kind of pressure he'd meant. He wanted her. She knew that as surely as she knew she needed air to breathe and food to eat for survival. Now she knew she needed physical intimacy with this man for her soul's survival. And somehow he knew she needed a little space first.

Some long-dormant instinct switched on. In a moment of crystal clarity she knew he was waiting for a sign from her, letting her make the first move. Something to let him know she was ready to take the next step. She wasn't afraid of him. She wasn't. If she said no, he would stop.

Please God don't let me freeze up, she prayed.

She walked over to him in the doorway and took his hand, leading him to the end of the bed. When his questioning gaze searched hers, she put her arms around his waist and rested her cheek against his chest. His heart beat strong and fast and she could almost hear it speed up with the closeness. Then he drew in a shuddering breath and tightened his embrace.

She didn't look at him, but let herself grow accustomed to his size and strength—his gentleness and consideration. "You've probably guessed that I haven't done this in a pretty long time."

His chest rumbled with laughter. "Yeah. I had a clue or two."

"About your expectations—"

He took her face between his palms and tilted her gaze up to meet his. "Don't go there, Katie. In my wildest dreams I never imagined being with you. If I had any expectations, they've already been fulfilled. All I want is to make you happy."

"I'm happier right now than I've been in a long time," she said with a small sigh.

His eyes darkened with intensity. "Would it make you happy to kiss me?"

She looked at his mouth, the firm, well-formed lips and remembered the pleasure they'd brought her just a short time ago. "Yes. I'd like very much to kiss you."

He took several shallow breaths through parted lips as he watched her, his muscles tensing. And she waited, bracing herself for him to do something about that kiss. It took several heartbeats before she realized again that he was letting her call the shots. He'd meant it when he said her wish was his command.

She stood on tiptoe and tilted her face up to his, anticipation making her pulse race. When her lips tentatively touched his, she heard his soft sigh as her eyes drifted closed. Their mouths rocked together for several moments, gentle and safe and sweet. He tasted of mouthwash and she realized he had been getting ready for bed. He just hadn't known bed would include her. And the thought elevated her trust in him even more.

He spread tender kisses over the undamaged side of her face, then caressed her eyelids and worked his way to the groove that marred her cheekbone. The kisses were soft—slowly and quietly stirring the fires inside her, spreading the warmth everywhere.

He took her mouth again and she heard another sigh of satisfaction. Hesitantly, lightly, he traced her lips with the tip of his tongue. Again instinct took over as heat began to build and she parted for him. He groaned as he dipped inside and she met his thrust, their tongues dueling, darting, seeking. Breath mingled, slipping back and forth until it was used up and they were forced to pull apart and draw in air before their mouths came together again.

The kisses went on and on in the muted light at the end of his bed. Each one was deeper, longer, more sensual and interrupted by his deep, masculine rumbles and growls that for some reason turned her insides to liquid.

Her breathing ragged, she pulled back and winced.

"What?" he asked sharply.

Her laugh was shaky. "Nothing. A crick in my neck. I guess we're incompatible heightwise."

"A challenge with an easy solution." He took her hand and led her to the side of the bed. He sat down and pulled her onto his lap. "Problem solved," he said, dropping his hands to his sides.

So there she sat, perched precariously. Through her robe, the muscular strength of his thighs settled against her backside. She looked at him and the heat in his gaze threatened to consume her. But she wasn't frightened because he was letting her take the lead and show him what she wanted. She realized she missed his arms around her.

She rested her arms on his shoulders and linked her fingers behind his neck. "Hold me."

"With pleasure."

Instantly his arms surrounded her, pulling her to him until an edgy, achy, dull throbbing spread from her center to her breasts. If only he would touch her there, but she didn't know how to take the lead on that.

As if he could read her mind, he moved his hands to her waist, then parted the V of her robe and hesitated. He was waiting for a sign from her. When she went completely still in anticipation, he slipped inside the material, feathering his fingers on either side of her breasts. She drew in a sharp breath the instant he cupped her left breast through the silk covering it. The contact zapped her like static electricity. His touch was warm and exciting and stole the breath from her lungs, making her feel weak with wanting.

"Nate," she whispered. "Would it be all right if we lie down on the bed? I'm going to slide off your lap and into a lump on the floor."

"I'd never let you fall."

Still, he stood with her in his arms and settled her gently in the center of the big bed. The tie on her robe was completely undone and doing nothing to preserve her modesty. Although she couldn't generate the will to care. There she was in silk lavender camisole and matching shorts—practically naked, but not quite—as their gazes locked just before he rested one knee on the mattress, then slid down beside her.

He braced on an elbow and studied her, a look of wonder mixing with the intensity permanently stamped on his features.

"What are you thinking?" she asked.

He blew out a long breath as he tucked a strand of hair behind her ear. His hand was shaking. "I'm thinking—"

"What?" she prompted, pressing her palm over his heart to feel the powerful thudding.

"I don't mean this in an offensive, macho way," he qualified.

"You're scaring me," she teased. "I promise not to be insulted."

"Okay. I was just thinking how good you look in

my bed. I was thinking that I'm the luckiest man on the planet. You're so beautiful."

He was lying; the mirror didn't. But, the expression on his face made her see through his eyes and she believed him. "That's probably the nicest thing anyone's ever said to me."

He grinned and she was grateful to be in a prone position because all her bones turned to mush while her heart began to race. Then he put his hand on her waist and lowered his mouth to hers. This time her mouth automatically opened, inviting him in and he accepted the invitation without hesitation. His tongue swept inside, teasing and caressing, creating a trail of tremors that traveled to her abdomen.

While he had her mouth occupied, he slid his hand beneath her top and up her rib cage, before tracing the fullness of her breast with his finger. She held her breath, but he simply circled the roundness over and over in a mesmerizing, arousing motion. His fingertip drew ever closer to her nipple. She squirmed and writhed, aching for the contact where she needed it most. When he finally took the nub and rolled it between his fingers, her body took on a will of its own and arched into his palm. And she realized something wonderful was happening. A hot aching heaviness grew deep inside her, in a place where she'd never thought to feel anything again.

When he slid her top over her head, she was grateful to feel coolness against her heated flesh. Then he kissed her lips before nibbling along her cheek, jaw and chin. He caressed his way to her neck and a hollow beneath her ear that was just this side of heaven.

Moving lower still, he kissed her chest before his mouth closed over her nipple and drew it into his mouth. Her breath caught as her fingers burrowed into his hair to hold him to her.

"You know," she said, her breath coming in gasps. "Turnabout is fair play."

He groaned deep in his throat as he lifted his head and met her gaze. Two heartbeats later, he'd whipped off his shirt and pulled her against him, skin to skin. "I don't think I've ever felt anything so good," he rasped.

The gravelly warmth of his voice burrowed deep inside and melted the block of fear she'd lived with for so long. She was in control. She could do what she wanted. And she wanted to run her hands over him, to see if he felt as hard and masculine as he looked. When she slid a hand between them and touched his chest, he groaned, easing onto his back, letting her have her way with him.

She touched the dusting of hair that spread across his wide, muscular chest then narrowed and disappeared below the waistband of his jeans. She caught his nipple between her fingers and gently rolled it as he'd done to her. His moan of pleasure made her feel powerful and in charge and she would be forever grateful to him.

She studied him and saw the bulge in his jeans that told her more than words how much he wanted her. Her heart started to pound but she kept repeating over and over to herself that Nate wouldn't hurt her. She was in control. And again the fear receded, making way for the need that grew into a pulsing ache between her legs. She wanted more. She wanted him inside her.

"I need you, Nate." When he stared at her, she knew he was asking without words if she was sure. "I need you," she repeated.

He nodded as he unbuckled his belt and slid off his jeans and briefs. His erection sprang free and she waited for the fear, but it never came. When he bent over her and pressed his mouth to her belly, she sucked in a breath. Then he slid his fingers inside her to coax and charm and ready her body for his. With one fingertip, he parted her and circled the nub of her femininity the way he'd traced her breast. Slower, closer he went until he touched the tiny core of nerves and the sensation was like a small electric shock that nearly lifted her off the bed.

Pleasure so intense she thought she'd die of it coursed through her and she arched against his hand. A mass of quivering sensation took over her body and mind, giving her freedom from doubt and fear. All she could do was feel as a series of shockwaves rippled through her. She went along for the ride, reveling in the intensity.

The release left her quivering, but she managed to open her eyes. "Nate, I—" She was embarrassed, and felt selfish. "You—"

He shushed her with a finger to her lips. "It's all right."

"No, it's not."

Years ago what was hers to give had been stolen. Now, freely and with everything she had, she wanted to give herself to Nate. He must have read that in her face, because his own turned dark with passion.

"I have a condom."

She didn't want to ask why. Or who he'd needed them for. Tonight was about the two of them. Only her and Nate. There were no yesterdays. Just tonight. The first night of the rest of her life.

She waited for him to retrieve the square packet from his nightstand and when he'd put it on, he pulled her close. He kissed her and somehow his touch ignited her own passion again.

"Now, Nate. I want you now."

This time he called the shots when he rolled onto his back and put his hands on her waist, helping her to straddle him. The feeling was heady and healing.

She slowly lowered herself over him, taking his flesh inside her, full and deep. The pain she'd expected never came because he'd made sure she was ready. With his hands on her hips, he guided her up and down, thrusting and retreating. Give and take, the beautiful way this consensual act between a man and a woman was meant to be.

Then he groaned, a sound that came from deep in his chest, before he threw his head back and shuddered with the force of his release. When he went still, she collapsed onto his chest, and he gently held her to him. Oddly enough, imprisoned by his arms she felt more free than she ever had in her life. It hadn't taken all the king's horses and all the king's men to put her back together.

She only needed this one special man to make her feel whole again.

Nate awoke with a start and felt someone beside him. The dim light from the hallway illuminated the slender figure cuddled into him and he breathed a sigh of relief. Katie's face was bathed in the finest GE glow. She sighed and nestled closer, settling her small hand on his chest. This has to be a dream, he thought. There was no other way to explain the girl of his dreams in his bed. If she wasn't real, he didn't want to know. He'd do his damnedest not to wake up.

Closing his eyes tight, he nestled her closer against him. The movement released a fragrant floral Katie scent from the sheets and he breathed in as it drifted around him.

What had he ever done to deserve this moment of pure happiness? What had he done to deserve Katie?

His college yearbook had outed him as the fraternity nerd. That secret was in the open and still she was here with him. But if she learned what he'd done at the frat house to alter the security cameras, he'd be lucky if she let him dig the mud out of her sneaker tread with a toothpick. And then there was how he hadn't lived up to all the good he'd planned to do. When he'd finally received his shiny new law degree and passed the bar, he'd been seduced by the dark side—by money and control—and he'd never looked back.

"Nate?"

He knew some people dreamed in color but wasn't sure about the current conventional wisdom regarding dialogue in dreams. The sound of her sweet soft voice and her silky skin pressed to his convinced him she was real. For that, he was more grateful than he could say.

"Are you awake, Nate?"

"Yeah." He smiled down at her. "Hi."

Her full lips turned up at the corners. "Hi. Why didn't you answer right away?"

"I was trying to decide if you were really here or just a dream." He shoved his free arm behind his head. "I can't believe Katie Price is here with me."

"I can't believe you're the same guy I knew in college. You look so different." She shifted away just a fraction and tilted her chin up to see him better. "Now that I remember you, I seem to recall your nose was crooked, too. Was it broken?"

"Yeah. I got it fixed along with everything else."

Except his soul. And the deep conviction that he'd tried and failed to defend her from Ted's bad-mouthing that night he'd popped him. If he had it to do over…

He wasn't going there; it was a waste of time. Life didn't usually give one the opportunity to do things over. That's why "put it behind you", "move on" and "get over it" were the buzzwords of the day.

"But it's not just your face," she said. "You're different. Everything about you."

"Is that a nice way of saying I'm not as beefy?" He hoped she was talking about his appearance and not his character. He hoped the black hole inside him wasn't quite so obvious.

"Let's just say that exercise equipment is doing an excellent job. You're in really good shape."

He laughed. "I'm brighter than the average bear, but I didn't know squat about physical fitness in those days. So I hired an expert."

"You mentioned the personal trainer."

"I could afford the best. Once I learned the basics

of exercise and good nutrition, I put effort into working out and eating right."

"With great success," she said, running her hand over his chest and abdomen. "I can't believe the difference."

"A healthy lifestyle is easier to achieve if you've got the money to pay for it."

"But are you happy?" she asked, studying him intently.

"I can't believe you're asking me that." He snuggled her closer. "I've got you beside me. What do you think?"

Katie Price was in his bed, her warm naked breasts pressed to his chest. Life didn't get any better. "I think in college, I fantasized about you—about this—and figured I was crazy."

"And now?"

"I'm probably the luckiest crazy guy on the planet."

She laughed. "I'm serious."

"I wish you wouldn't be."

"Okay. I'll be curious instead." She propped her arms on his chest and linked her fingers as she stared at him. "The subtext of my question was whether or not money makes you happy."

He smiled at her as he cupped her cheek in his palm and brushed his thumb over her scar. "I'd have to say definitely yes. At this moment, I'm happier than I've ever been in my entire life."

"In my case, money didn't buy happiness," she said, taking his hand from her face and lacing their fingers together again.

"Tell me honestly. If I hadn't reinvented myself—

if I was the same flabby geek with the broken nose—
would you be here now? Like this?"

"That's not a fair question. I don't know what I'd
have done."

"You just confirmed my suspicions. So I have to
conclude that money does indeed purchase happiness."

"I can't buy into that. No pun intended," she said.

"Why's that?"

"Your looks aren't all that's changed about you."

The familiar knot tightened in his gut. "What do
you mean?"

"The man I remember was sweet and shy and eager.
I don't recall you being so cynical."

"Hmm. Cynical? Distrustful of human nature. If
anyone has reason to be suspicious, it's me."

"I agree. Some—some people made life rough for
you in college. And yet, back then, you weren't cynical. I can't say the same now."

A lot of years had passed since he was that green,
inexperienced guy. And he'd spent most of those years
defending losers. He'd spent time meeting clients in jail
cells and police holding areas. Had the bad stuff rubbed
off on him? Had he become like the offenders he spent
time with? It was one of those offenders who'd taken
everything from her. Nate knew he had no business
being here with her, like this. He'd never forgive himself if the ugliness in his life touched her in any way.

Nate cupped her cheek again. "I think this comes
under the heading of Takes One To Know One."

She lifted a slender shoulder. "I plead the fifth,
counselor."

When she tried to look away, Nate gently urged her

face up to meet his gaze. "If I had the power, I would wave a magic wand and make your world perfect."

"If only…"

"If I had the power," he repeated, "I'd make your world safe and trauma proof. No ugliness would ever touch you again."

"There's too much ugliness in the world," she said. "No one can protect anyone else. Not completely."

Nate saw the pain in her eyes. He remembered her as a bright, eager young woman. He recalled the night she'd broken up with Ted and cried in his arms. Before that night, the girl he remembered hadn't been so cynical, either.

Guilt sliced through him when he thought about buying his lifestyle with the money he'd made defending the scum who do the bad stuff. Like the guy who'd used his car on Katie as a lethal weapon because he'd had too much to drink.

Everyone had regrets; no one got through life without them. But Nate wished for that magic wand and extreme makeover on his character. What a paradox. The man he'd been was good enough for her, but she practically admitted she wasn't attracted to him. Now he looked good enough on the outside, but the choices he'd made tainted his spirit. He might have been able to be both things to her once, but when he'd come to the fork in the road, he'd picked the easy way.

Now the damage was done.

He realized Katie had been quiet and when he looked at her he saw that she'd fallen asleep again. His heart caught at the sight of her—so fragile, so beautiful, in spite of what she thought about her scarred face.

He would do anything to protect this woman for the rest of her life. But it wasn't his right, and she was only here for a little while.

He smiled when it occurred to him that she hadn't changed so very much. She was still caring and kind. In spite of her limited resources, she'd put her problems on hold to come and do whatever she could for the professor. Then she would go.

If, by some miracle she stayed, there was no way he could keep the truth from her about what he'd become and she would know he wasn't good enough for her. When that happened, she'd run faster than you could say Quasimodo. So, for all the changes that had happened over the years, for him one thing hadn't altered.

Katie Price was, and always would be, out of his reach.

Chapter Ten

Kathryn walked into the kitchen where Nate sat at the table with the morning paper and a cup of coffee. She hadn't thought she'd made a sound, but he looked up and grinned the grin that made her good leg as weak as the one patched together with pins and plates and screws.

"Good morning," he said. He was trying to be subtle, but it was obvious he was assessing her to see if she was okay after last night.

"Yes, it is a good morning," she said, smiling to reassure him.

"How did you sleep?"

It was an innocent question. The polite thing to ask in the morning. Yet it was so much more than that. She made love to a man. She'd spent the night in his bed afterward. That was huge for her. She was accustomed to sleeping alone and should have been restless and uncomfortable.

"I slept great," she said truthfully. "Better than I have in a very long time."

"I'm glad to hear it." He took a sip of his coffee, then asked with deceptive casualness, "Do you think it was the exercise?"

Her mouth twitched with amusement. "I doubt it."

"No?" He put his mug down. "Because I've heard that exercise is a therapy for insomnia."

"Lucky for me I don't have insomnia."

"Not lucky for me." He stood and walked over to her.

Her heart started a staccato hammering as she anticipated his kiss. They were lovers now. And she was grateful to him for his consideration of her. But she didn't think she was ready for the next step. Her life was a mess.

"Nate, I…" She twisted her fingers together. "I'm not sure if—"

He reached for the pot on the automatic coffeemaker. "Would you like some?"

"Yes."

He took a mug from the cupboard and poured the rich, dark steaming liquid into it. "Cream and sugar?"

"Yes."

He took a container of fat-free half and half from the refrigerator and set it beside the sugar bowl. "I'll let you do the honors."

"Okay."

He moved out of the way, but stayed within arm's

reach, leaning his back against the island in the center of the kitchen. He slipped his fingertips into his jeans pockets and watched her.

"Katie, I was teasing about not getting lucky. I guess that remark was in poor taste."

She looked over her shoulder and saw the wrinkle on his forehead that meant he was worried. Putting the spoon on the granite countertop, she turned to face him. "I don't feel bad, Nate. Honestly. I feel wonderful. You were wonderful. Last night was—"

"Wonderful?" The corner of his mouth quirked up.

Sparks of awareness arced down her spine and stirred the embers inside her. They said the road to hell was paved with good intentions. In her case it could be the road to heaven, but she wasn't sure. She only knew if he touched her, all the good intentions in the world wouldn't prevent her from taking the journey with him. Now that the barriers were down, and she trusted him so completely, it would be easy to make a mistake. Now that she knew his past and remembered what he'd been through, she knew his humor and charm were a defense mechanism. She simply wouldn't take the chance of hurting him.

"It's just that… I know I'm the one who initiated… everything last night. But—"

"There's that word. I told you you'd hate me in the morning," he reminded her.

"No, Nate." She reached out a hand, then let it fall to her side. It was just as dangerous for her to touch as be touched.

"I'm sorry. I thought—"

"It's not about you," she protested. "Nothing about

you. It's me. I just don't think it's wise to start something we can't finish."

He stared at her thoughtfully for several moments. "I completely agree with you."

"You do?"

"Yes." He nodded emphatically.

Her eyebrow rose. "This isn't some lawyer trick, is it? Some reverse psychology thing?"

"Absolutely not. I'm just trying to be a nice guy."

And it was so working. It was time to change the subject. Thirty seconds more and she would follow him anywhere, including his bedroom.

"Okay." For the first time she noted he was casually dressed in jeans and knit shirt with collar and logo of an upscale men's designer. "Is this what the well-dressed attorney wears to work?"

"Only if he's having a midlife meltdown. I'm taking a couple days off."

"Not on my account, I hope."

He shook his head. "I've got time coming. I finished a difficult case not long ago and I—" He frowned for a moment, then looked at her directly. "I need a break."

"Okay. How about I buy you breakfast?"

His eyes widened as his whole body seemed to go still. "At a restaurant?"

"Yes."

"In public?"

"Yes."

"Are you sure?"

She was nervous. That much she was sure about. But he would never know what a difference last night had made for her. With his tender care, she'd found the strength to get over a hurdle that had dogged her for years. She felt empowered to move forward with a tentative step to take back her life.

"I'm sure," she said.

"I know just the place."

"This place is charming."

"The food is good, too."

When they were seated in a corner booth, Kathryn glanced around the small diner filled with people and was grateful that the hustle and bustle made her feel anonymous. That and the fact that her left side was facing the wall and hidden from public view. The floor was made up of alternating black-and-white squares. The red leather swivel chairs on shiny metal pedestals at the counter were all full. The table between her and Nate was gray Formica and the booths were covered in the same red faux leather.

"I'm starving," she said, realizing it was true.

"Me, too." But he was looking at her mouth. Quickly he took two menus that were braced between the wall and the metal napkin holder and handed one to her.

"Thanks." Her cheeks were warm as she tried to focus on the food choices inside.

"Can I get you guys some coffee?"

Kathryn looked up at the impossibly young and very pretty waitress. "Yes."

"Hi, Nate," the girl said.

"Hey, Christie. How've you been?"

"Good." She stared curiously at Kathryn. "Have you been in here before?"

Nate glanced at her, too. "No. She's a friend from California."

"I'm Kathryn," she said.

Nate cleared his throat. "Christie, I haven't seen you for a while."

She shrugged. "I've been busy. I had an interview last week with a top modeling agency."

"I didn't know you wanted to model." He glanced across the table at her.

"I've always wanted to. Ever since I was a little girl."

Kathryn wondered if she'd ever been so young and innocent. She couldn't remember. Beauty pageants had been a part of her life ever since she could remember and she didn't know whether or not it had been her choice. But somewhere along the line she'd felt as if the decision was taken out of her hands. Fortunately she'd had some college before her career started.

"It's not an easy life," she said. "Are you in college?"

Christie shook her head. "I don't want to waste the time."

"An education is never a waste," Nate said.

"But I only have so long to make it and a little bit of time while I'm young enough to be in demand." She stared at Kathryn. "You look familiar. Are you sure you haven't been in here before?"

"I'm ready to order," Nate interrupted. "What about you?"

"Me, too," Kathryn said, grateful he took the focus off her. She looked down at the menu, letting her hair fall across her face.

"Who's cooking today—Eddie or Sal?" he asked.

"Eddie."

"Then I'll have a number five. Fruit instead of hash browns and wheat toast."

"The vegetarian omelet," Kathryn murmured, reading the description of number five from the menu. "Make that two."

"Coming right up," Christie said, scribbling on her pad. She frowned, studying Kathryn again before she stuck her pencil behind her ear and walked away.

When she was gone, Nate said, "You okay?"

"Fine. You?"

"Yeah, but this is my turf."

"I guess if you know the cooks by name." She arched an eyebrow. "Vegetarian?"

"I'm secure in my masculinity. I refuse to apologize for not getting the meat lover's special, guaranteed to boost your cholesterol in a single sitting."

"Next you'll be telling me you eat quiche."

"Spinach," he agreed with a grin.

Their bantering back and forth relaxed her and she was really enjoying herself. Then the waitress arrived with their orders and they ate in silence.

When he finished, Nate glanced at her plate, then met her gaze. There was a bemused expression on his face. "I don't know where you put all that food."

"I can't believe how hungry I was. My appetite has been—less than robust for a while now."

"You could afford to put on a few pounds."

"That's something a model doesn't hear very often," Kathryn said, just as Christie arrived with their check. "At least not this model."

She snapped her fingers. "That's it. I knew I recognized you. Didn't you used to be Kathryn Price?"

"She still is," Nate said angrily.

"I'm sorry." Christie blinked. "I didn't mean anything. It's just that I want to *be* her." She looked at Kathryn. "A year ago everyone in the business was talking about you. You were the new 'type.' All the agents were looking for the next Kathryn Price." She caught her lip between her teeth. "You're so beautiful. You were on your way. No one knows why you disappeared."

Nate's glare stopped the flow of words. "It's no one's business. Can I have the check?"

"Sure. I didn't mean anything. Sorry, I—" Her gaze darted between them, then she turned away.

Nate tossed some money on the table and they quickly left.

"Are you okay?" he asked as they walked to his car.

"I'm trying to decide."

She was a little pleased someone remembered her. Definitely there was a nice big glow inside her at the way Nate rushed to her defense and played her champion.

"I'm sorry, Katie," he said as they stopped beside the car parked in the lot behind the diner.

"You have nothing to apologize for. It was my idea to go out. Of all the diners in all the world, what are the odds I'd walk into this one and be recognized?"

"When your face is all over TV advertising and magazines, the chances are pretty good. In fact, I'd say they're one hundred percent." He shot a glare over his shoulder at the offending building. "Used to be Kathryn Price," he fumed.

"She's right in a way."

"You're still Kathryn Price."

"And just who is she?" She leaned against the side of his BMW and folded her arms over her chest. "The Kathryn Price I knew died in that accident."

"Don't ever say that." The anger in his voice vibrated between them.

"It's true. The woman who survived is someone I don't know. And do you know what the worst is?"

"What?"

"Kathryn Price has nothing to show for herself."

"That's not true—"

"It is," she insisted. "I haven't done anything. My face is all over the place, but I haven't helped anyone. Not like you."

"I can't hold a candle to you. You're the same kind, caring woman I knew in college. Except now you're stronger. And you want to know something else?" He leaned his palm on the trunk of the car beside her.

"What?"

"Seeing you again, learning what you've been through—" He ran his hand through his hair. "You make me want to be a better man."

"Oh, Nate." She put her hand on his arm, feeling the warm skin beneath her fingers. "You are now and always were a good man."

"No, I—"

She touched a finger to his lips to silence him. "Thanks to you I've stopped focusing on what I lost. You've made me see it's time to look at what's next."

He shook his head. "You'd have done that in spite of me."

"You're wrong." She tilted her head to the side and smiled. "Thank you, Nate."

"I've done nothing to deserve—"

She stopped him again. "Just say 'you're welcome.'"

"You're welcome," he said, grinning.

There it was again, the sexy expression that should be registered with the romance police as a lethal weapon. The same man who'd made her look at what comes next could also be dangerous to her heart if she didn't watch out. Now that she remembered him from college his soft spot for hard-luck cases made perfect sense. But that inclination to get her back on her feet was far different from caring about her on a personal level. She didn't even want to think the word *love*.

But there it was. She'd been completely serious when she said the Kathryn Price she used to be died in that accident. Nate might have been able to love her. But he couldn't love the woman who'd survived.

Nate sat down across the restaurant table from Professor Harrison. "Thanks for meeting me."

"You said you were buying," the man teased.

Nate laughed. "I did."

"And you know how I like this place."

Nate looked around. He'd forgotten until this moment. But the professor had bought lunch for him many times at this deli. Red-and-white-checkered cloths covered the tables. They were sitting in the outside patio area enclosed by shrubs for privacy. The summer day was warm and humid, but a breeze kept it from being uncomfortable. When the college-age waiter appeared, they ordered turkey sandwiches on wheat. Nate wanted iced-tea and the professor his signature glass of Cabernet. Nice to know some things didn't change.

"How's Kathryn?" he asked, sipping his wine.

When he'd called the professor to set up lunch, Nate had mentioned she was staying with him until the meeting with Alex Broadstreet. That was about a week away and he felt time was his enemy, in every aspect of his life pretty much.

"She's well."

"How is she dealing with her—situation?"

"You mean the scars," Nate clarified. He shrugged. "I don't know. She's still struggling. The career she knew is over. And so much of our identity is tied up with what we do for a living."

So what did that make him, he wondered.

"So, what did you want to talk about?" the professor asked.

It was as if the man had read his mind. He looked up. "Kathryn," he answered simply.

"I need more information."

"Specifically, I'm confused about her."

"In a legal sense? Or are we talking about romantic issues?"

"Romantic. Maybe." Nate ran his fingers through his hair. "I don't know."

"Do you have romantic feelings for Kathryn?"

"Maybe. I don't—"

The professor held up a hand. "That's an unacceptable answer. Of course you know. And the answer is yes or you wouldn't be buying me lunch."

"Busted," Nate admitted sheepishly. The man was still sharp. That hadn't changed, either. "The thing is, I could stop caring now. Just shut it down."

"Why would you want do that?"

"Because she doesn't know about me."

"Define 'know about me.'"

"There's a rumor of a sex tape of Kathryn from the frat house. She dated Ted Hawkins and he was involved in that scandal—"

The professor made a dismissing noise. "He's a cretin. Who would believe a word from him?"

"That's what Sandra said."

"Ah. Ms. Westport."

"Yeah. We can talk about her later."

"Indeed."

"The thing is, Professor, if there is one and it comes to light, Katie has no clue that I'm the one who rigged the security cameras at Alpha Omega to film in the bedrooms. They told me it was for security. To protect the fraternity from lawsuits."

"So you had no idea how the cameras were going to be used." It wasn't a question.

"I'm glad you believe me. But will Katie? Especially when you put that together with what I do for a living."

"You're an attorney." He took another sip of wine and patiently waited for more details.

"I defend criminals. I take the side of bad people against the good guys who are trying to keep them off the street." He sighed. "All she knows is that I'm a lawyer. I never told her my specialty."

The professor frowned as he took the stem of his

wineglass and slowly twirled it. "Everyone has secrets, my boy."

Nate wondered about that look and the cryptic remark. He'd told Katie that where there's smoke, there's usually fire. "Everyone? Even you?"

He looked up. "Even me."

Nate felt a pressure the size of Rhode Island in his chest. "Like what?"

"Have you ever done the wrong thing for the right reason?"

"Probably. Although for me it's more like the right thing, wrong reason."

"Only with time can one gain a perspective on one's actions. When events unfold, that's when one wonders if the good of the one outweighs the good of the big picture."

Nate shook his head. "That was clear as mud. What are you trying to tell me?"

"I wonder if I made a mistake."

His bad feeling just expanded—Texas size. "Are you talking about me? Am I the mistake?"

"They say confession is good for the soul. And I can't help wondering now that I see you again." He sat up straighter. "Do you remember missing my classes? Family emergency, I believe."

He'd never forget it. His grandmother had needed him and he owed her everything. "Yeah. I remember."

"You were in danger of failing two courses. Not because you couldn't do the work. Quite the contrary. You didn't even need to show up for lectures to do well. The problem is the university standard states that student absences directly impact a grade."

"But I aced the finals in those classes."

"You did. And that would have been enough to pass. But because of your excessive nonattendance, your grades should have been lower."

Nate stared at him. Suddenly the professor looked far older than his years. "Are you saying what I think you are?"

The older man looked troubled. "I changed those two grades. If I hadn't, you'd never have been accepted into the best law school in the country."

Nate felt as if he'd been poleaxed. The professor had lied? For him? But he realized that on some level he'd always known. He'd been aware of the rules but never questioned his good luck. He'd simply been relieved about his grades and went merrily on his way because he didn't want his suspicions confirmed.

What did that make him?

"I see that you haven't completely mastered the art of hiding your feelings. I've shocked you."

"Yes. And no," he admitted.

"You see, I was always fond of you, Nate. You didn't have a father figure in your life and I took a shine to you. I knew you had your heart set on that particular school because it was a bridge to success. And money, which was very important to you as I recall."

"It is when you don't have it." And you can't pay for the most basic important needs.

"Yes." The professor frowned. "At any rate, now that I see how things have turned out for you, I can't help wondering if I've done you a disservice."

That makes two of us, Nate thought. His career was

based on deception? Again he wondered what that made him. A co-conspirator? Accessory to the crime?

But now it made sense that he'd so easily aligned himself with cheats and liars. He was one of them.

"I don't know what to say," he admitted. "And it doesn't help with my original problem. In fact, it's worse," he said, anger humming through his voice. "Someone as sweet and kind and good as Kathryn won't give me the time of day if she finds out what I am."

"Is that really who you are?"

Nate stared at him. "Isn't it?"

"You didn't start out to be a criminal defense attorney. The innocent, eager, young man I remember who wore his heart on his sleeve was going to defend the downtrodden. As I recall your goals were lofty. Exceptionally noble."

"Yeah."

Nate's anger drained away as he realized what the professor had done wasn't to blame for the path he'd chosen. Everyone had to take responsibility for their own actions. Speaking of which… If the professor had changed Nate's grades, what had he done for his other students? Where there's smoke there's fire. He didn't want to believe there was any merit in the board of directors investigation. But what if they had something on him?

"Lofty goals. Noble." And he'd done nothing with them. Nate met his gaze. It was time to change that. "I'm meeting with Alex Broadstreet in a few days. What am I going to say? Is there anything else I should know about?" When the professor started to speak, Nate held up his hand. "It's better if I don't know.

What you did for me was one incident. It shouldn't wipe out all the good you've done."

"Good?" His expression was ironic. "I'm not so sure. You're dissatisfied with your path—"

"But I chose it," Nate said. "Is it right or wrong? I suppose the fact that I don't want Katie to know answers that question."

"It's never too late." His smile was thin. "Again I seem to be quoting clichés."

"I don't know about that. And you don't need to be worrying about me right now. You need to think about yourself."

"Yes."

"If it's any consolation, I went through some records for Sandra Westport and couldn't find anything incriminating. That's a good thing."

"Speaking of good things, did you know Sandra and David want to purchase the empty building next to their store and turn it into a sports camp for children?"

"She said something about that."

"They're working on a written proposal of their intentions and she's asked me if I would give it to the benefactor. They're hoping he'll buy the building."

"If he does, the mystery of his identity could be solved. His name would be on title papers and become public record," Nate pointed out.

The professor shook his head. "He's given me power of attorney to do this one transaction."

"So he's going to help?" Nate asked.

"Yes, I believe he is."

"Did Sandra tell you that they've asked Katie to be the celebrity spokeswoman for their venture?"

The other man nodded. "She mentioned it. They were hoping she would share her knowledge of public relations and fund-raising, using her experience as a model and public figure. But that part of their plan is on hold because of what happened to Kathryn."

"It's a worthy cause," Nate said.

"And it would be good for Kathryn."

"I couldn't agree more."

The professor's gaze grew doubtful. "And what's good for you, my boy?"

"That's a good question. And, right now I don't have an answer."

"Take it from me, the past doesn't stay there."

"What do you mean?"

"Just that secrets have a way of not staying secret."

Nate knew this man. He was advising him, trying to tell him something without influencing his decision. Either Professor Harrison wasn't as subtle as he'd been years ago, or Nate had simply matured and grown smarter and more perceptive.

Because he knew what he had to do.

He didn't know where this thing with Katie was going. But if it built into something, he wanted that something to be strong. And it wouldn't be if it was based on a web of lies. He was going to tell her everything—exactly what he did for a living. He'd confess that he'd recently defended Ted Hawkins in court and he would admit to rigging the fraternity house cameras.

Why did things always come in threes? The Father, Son and Holy Spirit. The Executive, Legislative and Judicial branches of government. And Nate Williams's major screwups. Any of them could sink him like a stone. All of them together meant he probably didn't have a snowball's chance in hell with Katie.

But the professor was right. Secrets didn't stay secret. The bad stuff would come out. It would be best if Nate did the outing himself.

Chapter Eleven

Kathryn was starting to worry. Nate had been gone for hours. In fact she'd found a note on the pillow beside hers when she awakened in his bed. She smiled dreamily at the memory of the night before and the way his hands and his mouth had made her body come alive and hum. Thanks to him, she felt like a new woman. Scratch that. He'd brought out the woman who'd been hiding and afraid of *being* a woman.

She looked at her watch and frowned. She was a new woman who was officially worried about him. His note had said he needed to go into the office and she should make herself at home. He'd also left his cell number, but when she'd tried calling, she'd gone directly to voice mail.

"Where are you, Nate?"

She paced the length of the family room. No one knew better than she that things could happen. Most of the time all was well but sometimes in a fraction of a second something occurred that changed your life forever.

She started to pick up the phone again when she heard the key in the door. Nate was home. Relief shivered through her followed by a warm thrill of anticipation as she hurried to meet him.

When he opened the door she said, "Hi."

"Hi, yourself." He looked tired and stressed.

Should she say something? Ask where he'd been so long? She was new at this—greeting her lover after work. She was new at being someone's lover and didn't know quite how to act, what the rules of behavior were.

"How was your day?" she asked, deciding on general politeness. That was when she noticed he was wearing jeans and a T-shirt, not exactly approved attorney attire for winning friends and influencing a jury. "I thought you were going to the office?"

He set his briefcase down in his study, just off the entryway. "I did, but just to pick up paperwork."

"Then—I see." She folded her arms over her chest as she leaned against the doorway. She'd barely managed to stop herself from asking where he'd been all day. Making love with the man the night before didn't give her the right to grill him like raw meat. But she did have the right to express honest emotions. "I was starting to worry."

He looked contrite as he moved in front of her. "I'm sorry, Katie. You should have called the cell."

"I did. And left two voice mail messages."

He pulled the phone from the holster on his belt and frowned when he looked at it. "I guess I forgot to charge it. The thing's dead."

"I'm glad I can't say the same about you."

He set the cell on his desk, then took her in his arms. "I went to see the professor."

That was a heck of a round trip. No wonder he'd been gone so long. Then a new worry kicked up. "Why? Has something happened with the college board? Is the professor in more trouble?"

"No. Nothing like that."

She stepped away from him and met his gaze. Something was bothering him. Shadows swirled in his brown eyes and the ever-present grin was conspicuously absent. In fact, his mouth was pulled tight and he looked tense. Ever since her accident, her world had crumbled, a piece at a time. Every time she'd thought she'd seen the worst, there was another blow. Bracing herself had become a survival technique and she did it now.

"What's wrong, Nate?"

It was almost as if she could see the wheels in his mind turning, trying to decide what to tell her. If he wanted her to go, all he had to do was say it straight out. But her heart caught painfully at that thought. She wasn't ready to go.

"Don't sugarcoat it for me. I can take it," she said.

His mouth turned up slightly at the corners, a ghost of his normal smile. "You're made of sterner stuff?"

"That's right," she said, lifting her chin. "Give it to me straight."

He took a deep breath and said, "I need a drink."

He walked past her and went to the buffet and grabbed the bottle of Jim Beam and the tumbler beside it. After pouring about half an inch in the bottom, he slugged it back with a shudder.

Whatever was on his mind couldn't be good if he needed liquid courage to get the words out. Maybe it would be easier on both of them if she simply disappeared.

"Nate," she said. "It was kind of you to give me a place to stay. But it might be better if I pack up and go home—"

"No!" He put his glass down on the buffet. His eyes were tormented as he met her gaze. "Don't go. That's the last thing I want."

"Okay." The expression in his eyes told her he was telling the truth. Leaving him was the last thing she wanted, too, and she was tremendously reassured that he sincerely wanted her to stay. So, whatever he had to say, she could handle it. "Then tell me what's bothering you."

"All right."

"Do I need to sit?" she said, attempting to break his tension with humor.

"Maybe." He ran his fingers through his hair.

"I was kidding."

"I wasn't."

Heart pounding, she sat down on the sofa in the family room, just on the edge, and folded her hands in her lap. He walked back and forth in front of her as if she were the jury and he was pleading his case. What could he possibly have to say that was so bad she needed to sit down?

Finally, he stopped pacing and looked at her. "You remember that I was in a fraternity in college?"

How could she forget? Ted had been a brother in the same one, Alpha Omega. She shivered as an instant memory of his cruel, handsome face popped into her mind. "I remember."

"Did you hear about the guys who were expelled from Saunders for taping sexual encounters at the fraternity house?"

Oh, God. She'd been kidding about sitting down, but now she was glad. She started shaking and knew her legs wouldn't hold her weight. She felt the color drain from her face and she went cold all over.

"Katie?" Nate knelt in front of her. "What is it? You're white as a sheet."

She shook her head. "It can't be true."

"What?"

"It's on tape?"

He took her trembling hands into his steady, strong warm fingers. "What are you talking about?"

She couldn't look at him. "I was sexually assaulted at the fraternity house."

"Oh, my God—" His eyes widened in shock, then his face went hard. "Ted?"

"Yes." A shudder started in her belly and vibrated outward until her whole body was shaking. Suddenly the words she'd held in for so long started tumbling out.

"H-he forced me— I met him at the house to tell him I was breaking up with him, that it was over between us. Th-then he cornered me in his bedroom. I—I said no, but he didn't listen. I t-tried to scream, but he covered my mouth. I—I tried to fight him, but he was too strong—"

"Katie… No…" His eyes closed for a moment as he shook his head in denial.

"Yes," she mumbled.

He surged to his feet. "That son of a bitch," he ground out through clenched teeth.

She barely heard the words or registered the fury in his tone. What that bastard had done to her was bad enough. Now to find out there could be a tape?

"I'd heard rumors about tapes, but I never really believed. I thought it was like an urban legend."

"No."

"Oh, God, Nate. If the guys responsible were expelled, what happened to the tapes? Are they still around? What if—"

His hands squeezed hers. "Don't go there."

"How can I not? What if it comes out? What if—"

"Look, it's been a long time and if the tapes haven't surfaced by now, chances are they're not going to."

"How can you be sure?"

"I can't," he admitted. "Here's the thing. The fraternity brothers involved could have been criminally prosecuted for what they did. But they never were. My guess is they cut a deal and part of it was turning over the tapes so they could be destroyed."

He was a lawyer. What he said made sense. If she hadn't been so upset, she never would have blurted out what happened to her. Now that it was out there, she couldn't take it back. Shame rolled through her along with the feeling of being dirty. She'd tried so hard to put that behind her, but even now the emotions threatened to drag her under.

She shook her head. "I don't want to talk about it."

"That night," he said, his voice vibrating with anger, "when I followed you from the house. You were upset and said you and Ted broke up. He hurt you. I thought you were saying he'd cheated on you."

She shook her head. "If only—"

"I wish I'd beaten the crap out of him that night." He stared down at her as fury etched his handsome features. "You should have told me then and there."

"I was too ashamed."

"It wasn't your fault. You were a victim. Did you ever report it?"

"I never told anyone."

"No one? Not your parents or a friend?"

She shook her head. "I thought it would go away if I could just get back to normal. But I've done a lot of reading about it. Many assault victims keep it to themselves for years, then something triggers the memories."

"Coming back to Saunders triggered it for you," he guessed, clenching his hands into fists. "I should have taken him apart— I'm going to make him pay—"

"Nate." She stood and put her hand on his arm. "Even if you knew how to find him, what good would it do?" Hostility radiated from him in almost tangible waves. "It's a crime of control and brutality. Violence doesn't solve anything. I don't need you to do that. It won't undo what he did. That night—" She waited until he met her gaze. "You did what I needed you to do."

"It was nothing. I held you while you cried. I didn't know—"

"Because I didn't tell you. Now they call it date rape. Or acquaintance assault."

He made a sound deep in his throat, an angry growl. "Stupid trendy terms to white-out the ugliness. It wasn't a date because you told him you weren't dating him anymore. That son of a bitch forced you— If I'd known, I'd never have—"

She touched his mouth with her fingers to stop the flow of his angry words. "Shh. It's over."

In a moment of absolute crystal clarity she realized it was the truth. A sense of relief and cleansing floated through her. It was as if by relating what happened, the burden wasn't so heavy because she had someone to share the load. But when she looked at Nate, the deep lines beside his nose and mouth, the intensity swirling in his eyes, the tension in his body, she regretted saying the words and wished she could take them back and spare him the pain.

She looped her arms around his neck as she looked up at him. His body was taut with tension. "I'm sorry, Nate."

"You have nothing to be sorry for. I wish I could take back what happened—"

"In a way, you did."

"I don't believe—"

"It's like coming full circle. You stayed with me and helped me through the worst night of my life. And when you made love to me, you gave me back the part of myself that was stolen."

"That night, when I saw you leave the house so

upset, I couldn't ignore it. You were there for me during a pretty rough time. If not for you, I'm not sure I would have made it. I owe you."

She felt his body relax a little. "Right back at you. I'll always be in your debt."

He put his hands at her waist. "Let's not debate the degrees of obligation."

"Okay. I can think of something much better to do."

Surprise chased away the last of his anger. He shook his head. "How can you want to—"

"Have you forgotten last night already?"

"Never. But—"

"Now that you know, you're afraid I'm too fragile?" She pulled his mouth down to hers. "It's in the past. You gave me a future. Let's make the most of it."

Instead of the sexy grin she expected, he frowned. "Katie, I don't think—"

She studied him. "Please don't do that."

"What?"

"Don't treat me differently now that you know my ugly secret." She searched his gaze for a clue about what he was thinking. "I'm glad it's out there." She felt him tense. "Running from it hasn't put it behind me. Now it's out in the open and I refuse to be sorry."

"But how can you want to— With me?" He looked desperate and she could only think about making that go away.

"I'm not afraid of you. I've never been afraid of you. You're the best thing that's ever happened to me. God's going to send me to hell for this and I'm sorry the professor is in trouble, but it's what brought me back to my roots. Back to you. Just like he said. I blossomed here once. I can do it again. With you."

"But, Katie, I need to tell you something—about me."

She shook her head. "It can wait. Don't you see? You've reawakened in me the feelings that most women take for granted. I never thought I'd be able to be with a man again. You gave that back to me. And I want you, Nate. So much."

"You don't know what you're asking."

"You're wrong. I know exactly what I'm asking." She smiled. "I promise I won't hate you or myself in the morning."

He sighed and pressed his forehead to hers. "You know I can't refuse you anything, don't you?"

"I do now. But I promise to use my power only for good."

She touched her mouth to his and felt his surrender. In his kiss there was an air of desperation and she wasn't sure what that was about. But it tugged at her heart. Then she forgot about everything else when their mouths turned into a hot and frenzied clash of lips and tongues and teeth.

She felt him tense, but this time it was more primal and primitive—an excitement and passion that heated her blood and stole her breath. He growled his satisfaction deep in his throat as he rubbed his lips against hers. When they came up for air, his breathing was ragged.

"You don't play fair," he said.

"Why whatever do you mean?"

"You've got that curvy little body and you know how to use it."

"Oh?"

"Oh, yeah. You've got yourself plastered up against me like we're skydiving and I'm the guy with the parachute."

She grinned. "You're the guy with the goods, all right."

He sucked in a breath as his eyes grew hot. "Lady, you can use your power on me anytime you want. I— I—" He slid his hands over her hips and around to her behind, squeezing and pressing her to him. He blew out a long breath. "You— I— Wow."

She laughed with the sheer joy of this moment. Was there anything that made a woman feel more like a woman than turning a man into a stuttering, staring, besotted, cute-as-can-be dope? She gloried in this moment—the sexy banter. The freedom to let go of her mental censor, to not wonder if what she'd said was a sexual come-on.

But it worked both ways. He'd turned her into a quivering mass of pheromones. His kisses drained her brain of coherent thought and made her blood snap and sizzle through her veins.

"Wow just about says it all. I think my knees just unlocked and are halfway to dissolve," she admitted, loving the look in his eyes that made her feel special.

"I can help you out there." He swept her into his arms. "I'm taking you to my bedroom."

"You must be a mind reader," she said against his lips.

"No. But you know what they say about great minds, same wavelength."

"I do."

Golden shafts of light from the setting sun broke through the partially closed shutters and gleamed on the warm beige walls of his room. He stopped beside the bed and removed his arm from behind her legs, letting her slide down his body. Her feet touched the ground, but she was still floating on clouds. She wanted desperately to feel her bare skin pressed to his, but as she lifted her arms to pull off her T-shirt, passion made her feel weak as a newborn kitten.

"I'd be happy to help you out with that," he said, a gleam in his eyes.

"My hero."

He grinned as he started to lift her shirt up and she raised her arms to help. Cool air fluttered over her hot skin as she reached behind to unhook her bra.

"Allow me." There was a smile in his voice.

She turned and in a heartbeat the scrap of material was loosened and in a heap at her feet. When his hands slid around and cupped the fullness of her breasts, her breath caught and she leaned her head back on his chest. She raised her arms again, this time clasping them around his neck, giving him the freedom to stroke her everywhere. He fed on her neck then moved to her shoulder as his fingers fluttered over her skin, touching, teasing, arousing.

This was wanton and so wonderful, she thought, praying the moment would never end. Then he dropped his fingers to the clasp at her waistband and with a quick twist of his wrist, opened it. In seconds, he'd pushed down her jeans and panties, leaving her naked in his arms.

She turned and let him gaze at her, from the top of

her head, over her breasts, down her abdomen. He frowned when he saw the scars on her leg, but she knew it wasn't about her. He was thinking about the trauma that had caused it. Nate had never expected her to be perfect. He'd always just expected her to be— well, just her.

She smiled. "One of us has too many clothes on." Instantly he started to pull off his T-shirt, but she stilled his hands with her own. "Allow me."

She pushed his shirt up and pressed her mouth to the muscled contour of his chest.

"You're going to kill me," he rasped, sucking in his breath. "And you know it, don't you?"

"I have no idea," she said innocently.

"I do."

And suddenly, almost at the speed of light, his clothes were gone. In a haze of desire, they tumbled onto the bed, a tangle of bodies as they struggled to touch and taste. He ran his hands over her from breasts to thighs, then dipped his fingers into the moist heat between her legs.

"You're going to kill me," he said again, groaning this time.

"No, I'm going to love you."

She pushed him onto his back and started to straddle him. He stopped her, then reached into the nightstand for a condom. After covering himself, he put his hands on her hips and guided her until she took him inside her and started to move.

"Oh, God, Katie—"

She couldn't respond. Her lungs were burning and her heart pounding painfully. She was drowning in sensation and need. Then he slid his hand between their joined bodies and found her point of pleasure. She rocked against his fingers, her breath coming in ragged gasps, heat spiraling out of control. Finally a bolt of pure pleasure arced through her and she collapsed onto his chest as the shockwaves followed.

When she finally stilled, he put his arms around her and settled her on her back without breaking contact as he began to move inside her. In a matter of seconds, he groaned and stilled and found his own release. He buried his face in her neck and sighed with supreme satisfaction. Pulling himself together, he left her and went into the bathroom. It was just a moment or two, but she missed his solid warmth.

When he returned to the bed and her, Katie let herself snuggle against him. She'd never experienced such closeness to anyone in her life. It had started with attraction, then she'd felt gratitude and now lust for this man. Add to that the warm glow in the region of her heart and it signaled trouble. Letting the feelings continue was dangerous. She was the first to admit that learning had sometimes taken her longer than it should. But life had taught her one lesson she'd learned the hard way and on the first try. The good things don't last.

And very quickly Nate was becoming not just one of the good things. He could be everything if she wasn't careful.

Chapter Twelve

After the waiter took their drink orders, Nate looked at Katie across the table covered with cloth, flowers, linen napkins and candles. He was nervous for her, out in public. If anyone gave her a funny look or curious stare, he wasn't sure what he'd do.

"So far Operation Covert Cuisine is successful," he said.

"I looked on the Internet. La Vie En Rose is supposed to be a really good restaurant. Thanks for bringing me here."

It hadn't been his idea. Unfortunately, he knew from personal experience that this particular place was a favorite of the rich and famous. He'd tried to talk her into going somewhere that wasn't the "in" spot. But she'd set her heart on coming here. How could he say no? She'd insisted it was finally time for her to grow a spine and stop hiding. She'd told him everything, then pleaded for Nate not to treat her like delicate glass.

He sensed that the confession had been healing and somehow liberating. But every time he thought about what that scumbag had done to her, he wanted to beat the crap out of that bastard.

"You're looking very fierce about something." Katie tipped her head to the side as she studied him. "I know you warned me that this was a high-profile place. But I think you're right that an early dinner will help us fly below the paparazzi radar." She frowned. "You're not upset about coming here, are you?"

He forced himself to unclench his fists. This was another makeover moment for her and he wasn't going to rain on her parade. "Of course not. This was where you wanted to go." He smiled. "Like I said last night— I can't refuse you anything."

She smiled shyly and if the light wasn't so subdued, an enticing pink would probably show on her cheeks. "And I promised to use that power only for good. This dinner is a symbol."

"Of?" he prompted.

"Progress. When I first came to Saunders from California, I was nervous as a long-tailed cat in a room full of rocking chairs. And that was just about leaving my hotel room." She held out her hands. "Now look at me. I'm having dinner in a restaurant—not room service or takeout. On top of that, I'm incredibly lucky to be with a very handsome man."

"I'm the lucky one. Every guy in this place is envious of me because I'm with you."

"Is that flattery? Or flirting?"

"No to the first, definitely to the second." He grinned, then glanced over his shoulder when the maître d' seated a couple in the booth next to them. He'd asked for a romantic table in the back, figuring it was more private. When he met Katie's gaze she was shaking her head.

"Nate, you're acting like a nervous stage mother."

He sighed. "You couldn't have said I look like an anxious sports dad?"

"The point is," she said, her expression wry. "You need to chill out."

"I'll try. I just hope we don't have another Christie-at-the-diner moment."

She shrugged. "If we do, I'll deal with it better this time. Thanks to you."

"I haven't done anything," he insisted.

"You're so lying. If not for you, I'd still be huddling in my room, a solitary recluse. A shriveled shadow of my former self. I'd only need a cat or ten to complete the oh-so-attractive visual."

He winced at the term "lying." There was that whole omission thing again. He'd had every intention of confessing his sins when he got home last night. Then she'd dropped her bombshell about Ted. How could he tell her he'd recently defended the guy on sexual assault charges? The good news was he'd lost the case. The bad: the appeal was pending.

"Earth to Nate."

"Hmm?" He met her gaze, then smiled wryly. "Sorry. I've got a lot on my mind."

"Not allowed," she said, shaking her head.

"Oh?"

"Not when I'm trying to thank you for everything you've done."

The waiter interrupted her, appearing at the table with a tray bearing drinks. "A merlot for the lady. A Cabernet for the gentleman." He glanced from Katie to him. "Do you need more time? Or would you like to order now?"

He wanted to eat and get the hell out of there, but he put on his "courtroom" face as he looked at her. "Do you know what you want?"

She nodded. "The halibut, please. With a salad."

"Very well," the waiter said. "The house dressing is excellent. And for you, sir?"

"The same."

"I'll bring your salads right away."

Katie's face glowed with excitement and he decided his worrying would only spoil this for her. He held up his wineglass. "I propose a toast. To new beginnings. And a successful test run tonight."

"I'm not worried." She touched her glass to his then took a sip and looked around. "This place is still pretty empty. I know from personal experience that anyone trying to get noticed shows up much later."

"I can't believe you had to work at getting noticed."

"Believe it." She smiled a little sadly. "In the modeling world, pretty girls are a dime a dozen. Success depends on standing out from the crowd. Getting your name and picture in the right gossip column. Or an entertainment segment on a prime-time magazine program. Being seen with the right person."

He was glad she didn't know she was slumming to-night. As a person, he couldn't be more wrong. "What did you do to get your name in the paper?"

"I left that to my publicist. He would 'leak' my whereabouts to the press so I could be photographed."

He reached across the table and put his hand over hers. "Do you miss it?"

She thought for a moment as she met his gaze. "Not as much as I would have thought. My biggest concern is what's next."

"Have you given up on the Westports' offer?"

"They wouldn't want me."

"I don't think they care about your face." He felt her flinch in the hand he was still holding. "That didn't come out right. Of course they care on a personal level about what you've gone through. But I don't think they would rescind the offer because of it."

"Are you sure?"

He nodded. "Sandra as much as told me the day we had lunch. Apparently you were 'glimpsed.' The scarf and glasses weren't enough to keep you in-cognito. As a matter of fact it was my paralegal, Rachel, who realized who you are. You still have the recognition factor and you have an opportunity to use it for good."

"I'm not sure what to say to that."

"Unlike me. I've been told I'm never at a loss for words. But in my profession, that's a definite plus."

"Is that a hint that there's something you'd like to say to me?"

"I said it before. Sandra knows your face isn't per-fect and that hasn't changed her mind about wanting you as the celebrity spokeswoman for the sports camp."

"Again—I don't know what to say."

"You don't have to say anything. There's no pressure, Katie. Just don't dismiss the idea without thinking it over carefully."

"Okay."

"Good."

Then, Nate turned the conversation to lighter topics and did his best to keep the smile on her face. The food was excellent and her company even better. After taking care of the check, Nate took her elbow and led her outside, then handed his claim check to the valet. While they were standing on the sidewalk, he heard the screeching of tires from the SUV parked across the street. It made a U-turn and came to a stop in front of them.

Nate had a bad feeling and instantly pushed Katie behind him, protecting her with his body as if automatic gunfire was imminent. When the car windows went down, bright lights flashed and popped. They were being photographed.

"Damn it." He started toward the vehicle and Katie held his arm.

"Don't make a scene," she whispered. "It'll just make things worse."

Anger churned inside him. How did this happen? It was what she'd been afraid of all along.

Just then tires squealed beside them and the valet jumped out of his car. Nate kept himself between her and the photographers, shielding her as best he could until she was safely in the passenger's seat. As he went to the driver's door, the cameras were aimed in his direction and the flashes nearly blinded him. And all he could think about was getting her out of there.

When they were safely inside the security of his building, they took the elevator to his floor and he let them inside. It was dark in the entryway and as they passed his study, Katie said, "It looks like you have a message."

He saw the red message light blinking. "I'll get it later."

"Might be important."

He shrugged, then flipped on the light as he went into the room and pushed the button for the message.

"Nate? It's Professor Harrison. I just wanted to warn you that Alex Broadstreet knows Kathryn is there with you. I—I'm sorry I let it slip. I guess he pushed all the wrong buttons—or maybe the right ones when I told him about all the support I'm getting from my former pupils. Anyway, I just wanted to warn you and Kathryn. I know she's vulnerable right now and I wouldn't put it past Broadstreet to do something to undermine my support base."

Nate's expression was grim when he looked down at her. "The creep must have leaked it to the press that you were at my place. The paparazzi staked it out then followed us to the restaurant."

She nodded. "Yeah. That would explain it."

He linked her fingers with his and led her into the kitchen. Then he poured them both a brandy. "I don't know about you, but I need this."

She didn't say anything as she took the snifter he held out. He threw back a slug of the liquor and waited for the heat to hit him in the gut. Then he met her gaze. "I don't think they got their 'money' shot."

She shrugged. "I hope they did."

"What?" He put his glass down and stared at her.

"If they did, I don't have to worry about it anymore. Do you have any idea what a relief that would be?"

He put his hand on her forehead as if checking for fever. "Who are you and what have you done with Katie Price?"

She laughed and the sound as well as the humor on her face made him feel better. "Considering that was my worst nightmare and I can laugh about it—" She shrugged. "That's pretty close to a miracle, Nate. And I have you to thank."

"No—"

"I was trying to tell you at dinner. I'm blessed to have you back in my life and I thought no man could make me feel that way again. I just wish—"

"What?"

She sighed. "That I knew what I was going to be when I grow up."

The subtext of her words meant she was leaving soon. He'd known all along, but apparently deep inside he'd hoped to convince her to stay. The thought burned through him and it had nothing to do with brandy. He was between a rock and a hard place. Damned if he did, damned if he didn't. He still needed to tell her everything. If she stayed, she'd find out and he needed to prepare her. If she left— Go, stay, it didn't matter. When she found out his secrets, there was every reason that she would hate him forever.

So he decided to gamble and wait just a bit

longer. He wanted time, just a little more to make memories with her before he had to tell her he wasn't one of the good guys. That he wasn't the man she thought.

Kathryn couldn't believe Nate had canceled his appointments for the day just because she casually mentioned she'd like to see some of Boston's attractions. In college, time and money had been in short supply. One out of two hadn't changed. Money was a problem again but she had plenty of time on her hands. Still, Nate was a busy attorney and his sweet gesture started a warm, gooey feeling sliding through her.

They were in Dock Square and while he was getting them a cold drink, she studied Faneuil Hall, a two-story brick structure with arched windows trimmed in white, a bell tower and a long rich history. The stately building gave her a sense of the past and for some weird reason promise for the future. Or maybe the sense of possibilities was all about Nate.

"Here you go," he said, returning from one of the vendors in the square with two soft drinks. He handed one to her. "Why don't we sit down with these?"

"Sounds good to me."

They found a wooden bench trimmed with wrought iron and Katie let out a long sigh when she took a load off.

"How are you holding up?" he asked, a concerned look on his face.

"I'm okay. Although I admit I haven't done this

much walking since the Nurse Ratched at physical therapy pushed me until I wanted to strangle her with my bare hands."

"Should I be worried?" He was teasing, but she could tell he felt bad. She was learning to read the understanding in his eyes.

"Let's just say it's a good thing my hands are full."

"Lucky for me."

"And I'm glad we skipped to the third day of Boston's Best in three days instead of trying to condense days one, two and three into today."

"Katie, you should have said you were tired. We could have stopped whenever you wanted."

"I'm fine. I'm teasing. Mostly. And I wouldn't have missed any of this. The USS *Constitution,* the North End and Paul Revere's house. And it was very cool, by the way, but for creature comforts I prefer the hotel. The Old Church—one if by land, two if by sea, and now this," she said, holding her hand out to indicate the historic building. "It's like taking a step backward into the beginnings of our freedom."

"Maybe that's why they call it the Freedom Trail."

"Wise guy," she said, playfully punching him in the arm.

"It's one of my finest qualities," he said with an air of innocence that made her laugh.

She stopped and stared at him. "I haven't laughed this much since—"

"When?" he prompted.

"College," she finished. "With you."

"Oh?"

"Yeah. After…that night…" She lowered her gaze

and played with the straw poking through the plastic lid on her soda. "I remember we hung out."

He shuddered. "No wonder you were laughing."

"Stop putting yourself down," she scolded. "That's when I really got to know you. Your sense of humor flourished without Ted around to constantly needle you."

A frown slid over his features and he stared into the distance. "Ted thought he could do whatever he wanted without consequences. He was a controlling, egotistical creep who thought his sweat didn't stink."

"He probably still is," she agreed.

"Yeah."

"But I don't want to talk about him. I want to talk about you."

He shifted uncomfortably as he briefly met her gaze, then let his own skitter away. "What about me?"

"I was just thinking that you were wonderful then, and you're the same man now." She pumped her straw up and down in her drink to troll for liquid on the bottom. "Even though your looks have changed."

"You think that would make me different?"

"Yeah. Most guys would turn into a jerk if they looked like you."

"I'm no big deal."

"You're so wrong." She half turned toward him. "But that's what I mean. You have the same, sweet, unassuming quality you had in college. You haven't changed." She frowned. "On the other hand, my looks *have* changed and not for the better."

"Katie, you're still beautiful—"

She put her hand on his arm. "I'm not fishing for

compliments. This is about soul-searching. I've had to really look at who and what I am since coming back to my roots."

"Just like the professor said." He smiled. "So what have you discovered?"

"It's not very pretty," she admitted. "When the going got tough, I reverted back to type and became shallower and more self-centered."

"Don't put yourself down," he said, paraphrasing her. "You had to be self-centered to get back on your feet. That took guts and determination."

"That's assuming I have both. And I hope you're right that I do because I'm going to need those qualities to change."

"Into what?" His eyes widened in mock horror. "You're not going sci-fi on me, are you?"

She laughed and shook her head. "I just want to do better. I want to change. Maybe work with kids. Become a teacher. I want to make the world a better place. Like you."

"I'm nothing special," he said, an odd edge to his voice. "But you can do whatever you set your mind to."

"I have to finish college. I dropped out right after my sophomore year. You went to law school and I just—" She hesitated, remembering the feelings of desperation, fear and futility. "Couldn't stay at Saunders. I decided to listen to my parents and find my fortune through my face."

He touched her arm. "You're so much more than just a face, Katie. You're beautiful on the inside. And funny and smart. All the things you said hadn't changed about me are true for you, too."

"Well, it's time I started using all my talents—whatever they are."

"I'll do whatever I can to help. I hope you know that."

She nodded. "Thanks. You've already helped more than you know. Like today. If not for you, I'd never have seen Boston."

"I didn't do anything but take the day off work."

She shook her head. "It's not just that. The fact that I'm out in public without a bag over my head is all thanks to you." He started to say something but she held up her hand to stop him. "Do you remember that nightmare I had at the hotel?"

"Yeah."

"It was just one of many." She frowned. "Sometimes I dream that I'm the way I was. Then I wake up and the real nightmare begins when I look in the mirror."

"Katie," he said, covering her hand with his own. Offering reassurance. Just being Nate.

"The thing is, I'm finding out that hiding doesn't work. People have seen me. Rachel. You. And the world didn't come to an end. I need to get out. I need to live. Let people see me. Go sightseeing. Be one of thousands who has a story and keeps putting one foot in front of the other. When you do that…" She stopped, searching for the words.

"What, Katie?"

"When you do that, normal happens. I've done the beauty queen thing, and I've seen my life flash before my eyes when I thought I would die. After that I faced the fact that life as I knew it was over. Now I desperately want ordinary, typical, common, average. And you made me see that I can have it."

"Talk is cheap. If anyone knows that, it's me. You're the one responsible for the makeover. You're the one taking the steps." He stood and held out his hand to her. "How about we take some together? Want to go home now?"

"Yes," she answered, putting her palm in his and savoring the warmth and security when his fingers enclosed hers.

He pulled her to her feet and continued holding her hand as they walked slowly to where they'd left the car.

Home. The single word evoked profound pleasure that bordered on pain. The thought of going home with Nate made her happier than she could ever remember. It was a feeling money couldn't buy. If anyone had learned that lesson, she had. The best things in life are free—like health, happiness.

And love.

But love was too much to hope for. She would need all the help she could get—including her guts and determination—to resist her growing feelings for Nate Williams. It had taken all the king's horses and all the king's men, not to mention trauma teams and physical therapists to put her body back together.

But if her heart got broken, there was no treatment on earth that could repair it.

After dinner Nate settled on the corner group with his arm around Katie and switched on a cable news show. He hoped she realized life didn't get any more normal than a couple watching television after dinner.

"Normal for me is watching the news."

"I never watch it," she said.

"Uh-oh. TV incompatibility." He looked down at her. "If I don't have up-to-the-minute news on, I feel out of touch with the world."

Her full lips curved up in a teasing smile. "The subtext of that statement is that you're a news junkie and I'm responsible for distracting you."

"In a good way," he said, unable to resist the lure of her lips as he dropped a kiss on her upturned mouth.

On TV, the voice of the reporter droned on in the background. "Now for entertainment news. We had a Nate Williams sighting."

Katie went stone still, then broke off the kiss and looked at the television.

"The high-profile defense attorney and bachelor-about-town was spotted at La Vie En Rose, one of Boston's best restaurants, in the company of a mysterious woman. The defender of the rich, famous and infamous refused to answer questions and left before anyone got a good look at his lady friend. This reporter has never known Nate Williams to be at a loss for words. What's up with that, Nate?"

He switched off the set then met Katie's confused, questioning gaze. "Good news. Your secret is still safe."

But his cover was blown big-time.

"They were photographing *you*. I was simply a fuzzy footnote to the story. So you're just a hard-working attorney?" She shifted away and stared at him. "I don't think so. Who are you, Nate?"

Chapter Thirteen

Nate had never needed his skills for pleading a case more. He had to make her understand why he'd kept the finer points of his profession from her.

"Everyone is entitled to a defense," he said. "That's why if you can't afford an attorney one will be provided."

"You got the fancy car and luxury condo from handling court-appointed cases?" she asked doubtfully.

"No."

He watched her fold her arms over her chest, instinctively protective body language. "I didn't intend to defend the rich and infamous. My goal was to represent the people who needed it most and could afford it least."

"They why don't you?"

"Ironically, it was my good grades in law school. I needed a summer job and a high-priced firm recruited me because of my GPA. It became clear that I had a talent for finding loopholes and spinning facts."

"I see." Her closed expression said she didn't at all.

"It's a multimillion-dollar firm and the money was like winning the lottery to a guy who never had any."

"I know better than anyone that money isn't everything."

"It is if you can't pay for medical care. You found that out, too," he said.

"My savings were wiped out, but—"

"You had enough to get the treatment you needed. My grandmother didn't." He ran his fingers through his hair. "She raised me from the time I was twelve and was all the family I had. When she got sick, all we could afford was a county facility where she was diagnosed with congestive heart failure."

"Oh, Nate—"

"With care and medicine, it's a condition that sounds scary, but can be controlled giving the patient many years of quality life."

"But?"

"In her case it was scary and killed her because we couldn't afford the prescriptions or ancillary services. She needed nutritional guidance, physical education to make her stronger, expensive diagnostic tests to determine the extent of the disease. A pricey procedure to regulate her heart rate. All of that would have prolonged her life indefinitely. At the very least it would have made her more comfortable. But we were poor and couldn't afford it. So I took care of her as best I could. And it nearly cost me everything."

"Why?"

"My college GPA was in the dumper."

"How? What happened? You're so smart."

"It was a couple of Professor Harrison's classes. Caring for my grandmother took time. I made it to all my other classes, but not his." He ran his fingers through his hair. "Now that I think about it, maybe subconsciously I knew he would help. Anyway, I aced the final because the subject matter wasn't a challenge. But there was nothing I could do about absences lowering my overall grade. That brings down the GPA, which limits law school choices. It's important to get into the best in the country."

"Did you?"

He nodded. "Thanks to the professor. When I went to see him the other day, he admitted changing my grades."

She gasped. "So you were right that where there's smoke, there's fire."

"Wrong thing, maybe. But you'd have a tough time convincing me of that. I didn't squander the opportunity."

"I'm sorry your grandmother had to go through that, but—"

"No buts, Katie. Money makes a difference. I didn't have it to help her. When I finally earned it, I was able to change my appearance. If I could have done it sooner, high school and college would have been good years instead of a time filled with bullying and—" He looked at her. "Never mind. The point is I saw a better life and I took it."

"But that reporter said you defend the infamous. I know I'm not the brightest bulb in the chandelier, but that means you represent people who commit crimes."

"Yeah." He stood and looked down at her. "Imagine that. Criminals have rights, too. Like all citizens. Today, when we walked the Freedom Trail, you saw where it all started. The patriots died because they believed in it enough to put their lives on the line."

"Yes, but I can't imagine that our forefathers wanted the bad guys to go free."

"I agree. But they wrote a Bill of Rights and a Constitution to protect the rights of everyone, not just the good guys." He put his hands on his hips. "It's my job to make sure my client isn't railroaded through the legal system. Almost every day there's a story on the news about someone wrongfully convicted and put on death row. Or the guy who spent seventeen years behind bars for a crime he didn't commit. No one claims our legal system is perfect. Far from it. But it's all we've got. And it's probably the best in the world." He took a deep breath. "I'm good at what I do. Defendants pay a lot of money for my services. It's my job to protect their rights and mount a vigorous defense. Anyone accused of a crime is entitled to that. To do less is cause for appeal."

Like Ted. His appeal was pending. It was a case Nate hadn't wanted in the first place. Then he'd lost it. Probably because deep down he knew the guy deserved to go to jail. The guy was a serial offender. Learning what he'd done to Katie confirmed his suspicions. On top of that, Nate knew his growing feelings for her, and hating Ted for what he'd done to her made representing the creep a conflict of interest. Ted was leaving him cell phone messages and he'd been ignoring them because he wasn't sure what he was going to do about that situation.

Katie moved to the edge of the sofa. "I just don't understand why you didn't tell me all this when we first ran into each other, Nate."

"The simple answer?" When she nodded, he said, "Because I liked hanging out with you."

"You're going to have to put a finer point on that."

"Last night the photographers were after me. When we ran into each other, if you had known that happens to me on a regular basis, what would you have done?"

"That's not fair. How can I know what I'd have done if you'd given me all the facts?"

"Come on, Katie. Be honest." He let out a long breath. "You made it clear you didn't want to be photographed. I figured out that you didn't have a clue who I was or the media frenzy that sometimes surrounds my cases. It wasn't a stretch to assume that if you knew I was hounded by the press, it would scare you off."

He looked at her, the big hazel eyes filled with doubts, the full lips he'd savored just a short time ago pulled into a straight line. Something shifted in his chest, something big, with the power to hurt. A lot. He'd lied by omission so he wouldn't have to let her go before he was ready. The hell of it was, after spending time with her, he wasn't sure he'd ever be ready to say goodbye.

"I am publicity shy since the accident," she admitted.

Okay. Good. She was being realistic. "The thing is, Katie. I didn't want you to be scared off. I wanted to spend time with you because I—"

"You what?" she prompted.

"I cared about you when we knew each other in college. I felt the spark when I found you again. I wanted to see what it was."

"And?"

He saw the pulse in her neck fluttering and hoped it was a good sign. "And, I found out I still care about you."

"I see."

That wasn't where he'd wanted to go. He hadn't wanted to tell her that. Not yet. He didn't like to veer from his game plan, not in court and not on a personal level. Not something this important. But he couldn't take it back. So now he had to do damage control.

"Look on the bright side," he said.

"Which is?" she asked, her mouth twitching.

"The photographers were after me. I took the heat. They only got pictures of me. You're still the mystery woman."

She looked down, and when she met his gaze again, a smile turned up the corners of her mouth. "I can't believe how you do that."

"What?" he asked.

He held his breath and hoped he'd made her understand. True, he hadn't wanted her to know how he made his living. And he had to deal with his crisis of conscience. But that was different from his feelings for her. Did she get it that he hadn't wanted to lose her before she got a chance to know him again? From that first moment, when he'd nearly knocked her down, he'd felt the stirrings of something deep and intense—feelings that had never died, but simply remained dormant. It certainly explained why he'd never completely connected with a woman. He couldn't and had a bad feeling it was because he'd been waiting for Katie.

But the professor had made him realize that he had no future with her until he put all his cards on the table. He still needed to tell her about Ted and rigging the security cameras at the fraternity house. Then his secrets would be out. All of them.

He drew in a deep breath. "Katie, I—" The doorbell interrupted. "Who the hell could that be?"

"Since this is a security building, I'm guessing it's not Avon calling."

"I've given the code to a couple people," he admitted. "None of them selling cosmetics."

"Hopefully trustworthy people." One of her dark eyebrows lifted.

The sassy look was a shot of adrenaline to his spirits. He'd cleared one hurdle. She'd learned the truth about his career and was still there. That wouldn't have happened when they'd first met. She wasn't as fragile as the woman he'd run into at the Paul Revere Inn. She steadfastly maintained that he was responsible for the changes in her, but the truth was, she had reserves of strength she didn't even realize existed. Sooner or later she'd have tapped into them and taken the steps. If he'd helped in any small way, he was glad. She hadn't run away and he clung to the hope that she'd understand everything.

"I'll just go see what the trustworthy person at my door wants," he said, cocking his thumb in that direction.

Kathryn smiled at his witty comeback as she admired his broad back and fine fanny leaving the room. Leave it to Nate to make her smile even though she was troubled by his revelations. He was an attorney who made entertainment news as well as court TV. Pacing back and forth in the family room, she tried to decide how she felt about that. Then she heard voices, just before he returned—with a stunning woman.

Nate held a file in his hand. "Kathryn Price, Rachel James. My paralegal."

Kathryn shook the hand the other woman held out and noticed it was small boned and delicate. The woman was a bit on the skinny side, not especially well endowed, but the rest of her was gorgeous. Halle Berry-like beautiful. She had flawless, café-au-lait colored skin and huge brown eyes fringed by long, thick, curly lashes. Her black hair was thick and shoulder length. She wore a conservative pin-striped pantsuit, a professional look, as if she'd come straight from the office.

"Nice to meet you," Kathryn said.

"Likewise."

"I'm sorry you had to come all the way over here, Rach," Nate said, glancing at the papers in his hands.

"If you'd pick up your cell phone, it wouldn't have been necessary." Rachel glanced at her. "Since he's been hanging out with you, he's almost impossible to get hold of."

Kathryn noted that the other woman's gaze was

frankly assessing. Then she remembered Nate telling her Rachel had glimpsed her scars. Glimpse being the operative word. If she'd been at all curious, now she was free to look her fill. To her credit, her expression didn't register shock, curiosity or pity. But her remark about Kathryn and Nate hooking up definitely oozed protectiveness for her boss.

"A man is entitled to some time off," he defended. "It has nothing to do with Katie."

"I'm just saying you've been unavailable for over a week now," Rachel said, her full mouth turning up in a teasing smile.

"Okay. You've made your point." Nate smiled, but it didn't reach his eyes. There was a grimness in the brown depths that hadn't been there moments ago. "Katie, I'm sorry. I've got to return a phone call."

"No need to apologize. I wouldn't dream of keeping you from your work."

There was a questioning look in his eyes, evidence of his not being sure about how she'd meant that. Which made two of them.

The grim look morphed into anger just before he turned and headed out of the room. "I'll be back."

"Yeah, him and the Terminator," Kathryn joked.

Rachel laughed. "That's not far from the truth. He's a force of nature in the courtroom."

Kathryn sat on the sofa and held out her hand, indicating the other woman should join her. "Does it bother you?"

"What?" Rachel sat about a foot away.

"That you work for a man who represents people who break the law."

"First of all, as Americans one of our basic rights is innocent until proven guilty. Second, not everyone who comes to Nate has committed a crime. They've been charged and it's up to the prosecution to prove wrongdoing beyond a reasonable doubt."

The flashing in the other woman's eyes was definitely all about protectiveness. "Okay. I stand corrected."

Kathryn noted her passionate defense of her boss and wondered if she had any romantic feelings for Nate. Again the sensation of jealousy sliced through her, a bad sign that she was a dismal failure at keeping her feelings for Nate under control.

"Look, Kathryn, I don't know what's going on between you and Nate, but I can tell you this. Years ago an innocent man was sent to jail for a crime he didn't commit because he couldn't pay an attorney's fee. That wouldn't happen today. At least the part about not having a lawyer because the law has changed. If a person can't afford one, counsel will be provided by the court."

"So Nate told me."

Big brown eyes narrowed on her. Rachel was shielding him like a mother lion looking out for her cub. "Did he tell you that even lawbreakers are entitled to have an attorney to navigate them through the legal system? The fact that it's his job and he does it well doesn't make him a bad person."

"I never said it did."

"You inferred," Rachel said, folding her hands demurely in her lap. "Nate Williams is a gifted defense attorney. He's also one of the finest men I've ever known."

"I'm sure he is."

"I hear a 'but' in your voice. Let me tell you a little story about my boss." She pulled in a deep breath and her eyes took on even more intensity for her subject. "My husband was sick for a while before he died and left me with a mountain of medical bills I couldn't pay."

Kathryn automatically reached up and traced the groove on her cheek. "I'm sorry that you lost your husband."

"Thank you."

"I understand the high cost of medical treatment. I'm in sort of a bind myself."

"You couldn't have a better person in your corner than Nate," she said vehemently. "The man offered to pay off my debt."

Kathryn's eyes widened. "He did?"

She nodded briskly. "Of course I couldn't let him. It's my responsibility."

"It would have been easier to take his help."

"Yes. But that's not the way I was raised. Besides, I loved my husband. I wanted to do it for him."

"I can understand that."

The words were automatic, because Kathryn had no clue how it felt to love someone that much. Although if she couldn't get a handle on her feelings for Nate, she was very much afraid she'd know before long.

Rachel leaned forward, obviously warming to her subject. "But Nate wouldn't take no for an answer."

Kathryn smiled. "I've noticed that about him."

"Yeah." Rachel's expression softened for a moment. "When I refused to let him write a check, he negotiated with my creditors to reduce the debt and worked out a more manageable pay schedule."

"You must be very grateful to him."

"I am. I'll be forever obliged and it's not a debt I can repay. If he's decided to help you, you couldn't be in better hands."

Kathryn shivered at the thought of being in his hands. They'd done magical things to her body, sensations she'd thought never to feel. "Yes. I'm finding that out."

Rachel met her gaze. "What happened to you?"

"Excuse me?"

"The medical bills?"

Kathryn gripped her hands in her lap, refusing to give in to the urge to touch the scar again. "Car accident. Drunk driver."

"I'm sorry. You're a model, aren't you?"

"I was." She met the woman's gaze. "Nate says you saw me and mentioned my situation to Sandra Westport."

Her gaze skittered away then, but just for a moment. "Yes. I knew she'd contacted your agent about the possibility of you being the celebrity spokesperson for the kids camp she and David are trying to get off the ground. When the offer was rejected, she didn't understand. When I happened to see you on that windy day, I got it."

Kathryn appreciated the fact that Rachel didn't skirt the issue. It was easier to talk about her face in no-nonsense factual terms, neutralizing the awkwardness factor. If only she could handle her feelings as well. Her first instinct was to run. And if it weren't for the fact that she had promised to do what she could to help the professor, she'd probably hop on the first plane back to California. But Nate had made her see that it was time to grow a spine and meet life's challenges head-on.

This encounter with his paralegal had proved he was right. From now on, every time a stranger asked what had happened to her, she'd be able to handle the question with more grace and less clumsiness. If not for him, she wouldn't have taken the first steps. Thanks to him, she was going to be all right.

"Nate has helped me in ways that money can't buy," she admitted.

Rachel smiled. "That's Nate. The guy in the white hat." She looked at her wristwatch and stood. "I've got to go, Kathryn."

"Are you sure you can't stay until Nate is off the phone?"

The other woman's gaze narrowed. "I have a feeling he's going to be tied up with that call for a while."

"I'll see you out." Kathryn stood and followed her to the entryway.

"Keep something in mind, Kathryn." Rachel opened the front door and hesitated. "If you're looking for reasons to convince yourself you're not in love with Nate, don't expect me to help you. He's a good man. You won't find a better one."

The other woman was gone before Kathryn could deny she was in love with Nate. She walked past the study, noting that the door was closed. She heard the sound of Nate's voice, but not the words. He was a big lump of contradictions, she thought, continuing on to the family room. She'd seen enough legal dramas to know that a defense attorney's job was to help criminals beat the rap. But Rachel and Nate had made her see that there was more to it than that.

How could she reconcile the man who helped the bad guys with the one who was a hero to his employee? And to her?

Was she going soft on him because her fascination had deepened into something she'd never experienced before? Something that would last a lifetime?

Hopefully not. She was just beginning to find herself. She'd made up her mind to take a big step forward and her plan didn't include getting serious. She didn't want to care about Nate because she didn't want to care that much for anyone.

Unfortunately, part of her makeover was not living in fantasyland. She needed to be realistic. And the reality was that she did care about Nate and fear was getting in her way. He'd made her see she needed to meet life's challenges head-on. How could she do less with what was happening between them? He might not want her. She might get hurt and never recover.

But, by God, she wouldn't have regrets.

Chapter Fourteen

Nate leaned back in his chair and stared at the pile of work on his desk. In his absence from the office, the files had multiplied like bunnies and he'd made little progress in familiarizing himself with current cases, motions heard and court dates pending. His concentration was out of whack thanks to thinking about Katie, sweet and sexy in her pink terry cloth robe. The good news? Job security. Bad news? Dealing with this workload would take a lot of time that he'd rather spend separating Katie from her fuzzy pink robe.

It wouldn't be long until she returned to California. The meeting with Alex Broadstreet was in a couple of days and after that she'd be gone.

He missed her terribly and it had only been a few hours since he'd seen her at breakfast. In the last couple of weeks, they'd been together constantly and just returning to work put him in Katie withdrawal. He could imagine how useless he'd be when she was on the other side of the country.

Unless he could pull a miracle out of his hat. A long shot since he still had a lot to get off his chest.

Last night if Rachel hadn't stopped by with the message to call Ted, Nate would have come clean about his whole life. The secrets would be out in the open, including the ones that involved Ted. Anger churned through him as he remembered his conversation with the arrogant bastard. Make it all go away, Ted had demanded. Nate wouldn't, even if he could. And rage at what he'd done to Katie had made it hard to think clearly. But hanging up on Ted Hawkins probably hadn't been the wisest course of action.

His secretary buzzed. He pushed the button. "Yes?"

"There's a lady to see you. She doesn't have an appointment."

"I can't see anyone—"

"She says you don't take no for an answer and neither will she."

Nate grinned. "Send her in."

The door opened and Katie stood in the doorway. There was something different about her. Shiny brown hair teased her shoulders and the light green silk blouse that covered them. Her dark slacks hugged her hips and thighs and accentuated her small waist. Black sandals revealed her red-painted toes. She was the same woman in the fuzzy pink robe that he'd left at his kitchen table a few hours before, but there was a sparkle in her eyes and an air of energy that was new.

"Hi," he said, standing.

"Hi. I hope you don't mind me dropping by."

God, no, he wanted to say, but simply shook his head.

She glanced around and walked over to the window. "Nice place you've got here. Corner office."

"Yeah. Law firms tend to give their partners the best accommodations."

"Terrific view," she said, scanning the city's skyline. Turning, she let her gaze wander over the furnishings, and stopped at his large desk. "Cherrywood is very lawyerlike."

"You think?"

"Yes. It has an impression of maturity and exudes trust. But it also reminds me of you—warm, confident, comfortable."

He looked at the office and tried to see it through her eyes. He'd approved everything and had liked the dark wood. Matching bookshelves lined the walls of the room and that was space for a lot of books since he had a lot of square footage. Paintings of seascapes and lighthouses filled in the empty wall space along with his elaborately framed college and law degrees. He took this environment for granted and didn't really notice it anymore. Seeing it through her eyes was one more reason to be grateful she'd stopped by.

"I can't say I'm flattered to be described as comfortable, though."

"Be flattered." She smiled and the promise in her expression made his heart pound, sending all the blood in his body to points south.

"What can I do for you?" he asked, unable to control the husky sound in his voice.

"You can let me take you to lunch."

"Lunch would be great." Better than great. Fantastic. Awesome. "But let me take you."

"I insist on taking you." She shook her head and the hair around her face swung with the movement, making his fingers itch to touch the silken strands.

Instead, Nate buried his hands in the pockets of his slacks. If he touched her, he'd kiss her. If he kissed her, the wanting that always bubbled below the surface when he was around her could boil over and scald them both. She was a classy, tangled sheets and thick comforter kind of woman.

"Is there any particular reason you insist on taking me?"

"We're celebrating."

"Oh?"

"I called Sandra Westport."

"I see." He walked around his desk and stopped a foot away from her—just close enough to inhale the fragrance of her perfume and savor the way it made his testosterone stand up and salute.

"I made an appointment to see her and David about their offer."

"You're going to be their celebrity spokeswoman." It wasn't a question.

"I'm going to discuss it," she clarified. She reached up and raised her fingers halfway to her scarred cheek, an automatic gesture. But this time she dropped her hand. "They may not want me."

"Not a chance." How could anyone not want her?

"I wish I had your confidence."

"They're going to love you." How could anyone not love her?

The *L* word surprised him. He'd never thought about her like that. Want, need, admire, but not love. In court he'd learned to plant the seeds of reasonable doubt in a jury's mind by suggesting alternate scenarios that were believable. But loving Katie? That had never seemed believable. Mostly, because he'd learned never to let himself believe. She was out of reach for a guy like him.

"I'm so confident they're going to love you," he said, "that I have an idea."

"Care to share?"

"When they make you a formal offer, tell them it needs to go through your attorney."

"That would be you?"

"It would. I can negotiate terms of the deal."

"And what would those be?"

"That a certain percentage of kids accepted to the camp be recovering from car accidents, or dealing with facial scarring, cleft palates, things like that."

"Oh, Nate." She clapped her hands together. "You're brilliant."

"All in a day's work."

"You're too modest." Her eyes shone with a suspicious brightness. "But truly, it's such a worthy undertaking. I can really do some good. And the weird thing is, I don't think I could have done the job right without having gone through trauma myself."

"Steel goes through fire and comes out stronger?"

"Something like that," she agreed.

He leaned his hip against his desk. "What happened to change your mind about calling Sandra?"

"You happened."

"Me?"

"You gave me a different perspective on everything. Any other man would have given up on me. But you hung in there."

"That's me. Nate, rhymes with saint. Almost."

"Hardly." She laughed. "You're a good, decent man."

"Even though I go to bat for the bad guys?"

"I'll admit there's a lot of gray area." She moved closer.

"Did Rachel talk to you?"

"She defended you most eloquently," Katie confirmed.

"I must remember to give her a raise."

"It's all about perspective. Between the two of you I realize life isn't just black and white."

"Especially where our justice system is concerned. Everything is subject to interpretation. That's why we have judges." He sighed. "You're not the only one who has a different perspective."

"Oh?" She looked surprised.

"For a while now I've been trying to reconcile what I do with my original altruistic intentions to represent the less fortunate. That was why I decided to study law in the first place."

"And?"

"Finding you again, knowing you…" He shrugged, searching for the right words, then reached out and took her hands in his. "I know I've told you this before, Katie, but you've made me want to be a better man."

"And?" she said again, squeezing his palms reassuringly.

"I've decided to take cases on a pro bono basis for people like you who have been wronged and don't have the resources to hire competent representation to make it right."

"Oh, Nate—" She dropped his hands and linked her arms around his neck. "We have even more to celebrate than I thought."

She stared into his eyes, searching, before she touched her mouth to his. The soft, sweet contact was like lightning to tinder-dry brush. Heat radiated through him and the blood roared in his ears, making it difficult to concentrate on anything but the woman in his arms who was engaging all of his senses. He thought he heard the buzzer on his desk and his secretary's anxious voice just before his office door slammed open. Katie jumped away from him and looked at the man in the doorway.

"What do you know? Wide Load Willie has a woman." Ted Hawkins smirked. "Getting a little at work is the way you're handling my appeal, Williams?"

"I tried to stop him, Mr. Williams." Nancy stood there twisting her fingers together.

"It's all right, Nancy. I'll handle this." Nate watched her close the door.

Ted looked Katie up and down. "Well, well, if it isn't my old girlfriend. How long has it been, Kathryn?"

All the color had drained from Katie's face and Nate knew she recognized the man who had hurt her in college. She was standing face-to-face with her worst nightmare and Nate had no one to blame but himself.

Kathryn stared at the man who'd stolen her sense of safety and trust so many years ago. What in the world was he doing here? Was this another Alex Broadstreet scheme? But this was Nate's office. And then she understood.

"He's your client." She looked at the man who'd given her back her sense of safety and shivered when the look on his face confirmed it.

She met Ted's gaze. He was still handsome—all wavy black hair and blue eyes set off by his tanned good looks, but there was no warmth in him. He was tall, fit and powerful and fear welled up inside her. But she wasn't running from anything any longer, not even him.

"How've you been, Kathryn?" He studied her face and winced. "Ouch. Don't tell me. I should see the other guy, right?"

Kathryn was determined he wouldn't get to her. Not this time. He couldn't control her now. "Why did you need an attorney, Ted? Don't tell me, let me guess. Sexual assault?"

His smile disappeared and cruel eyes narrowed. "It's my word against hers."

"He said, she said." She lifted her chin and looked him straight in the eye. "My money's on her."

"There's a surprise."

"It shouldn't be. I have firsthand experience of exactly how much you can be trusted."

"Are you accusing me of something?"

"Yeah. You assaulted me ten years ago. There's no doubt in my mind you're guilty."

"You wanted it, Kathryn." His mouth twisted with the ugly words. "Don't deny it."

"I said no. You forced me. Nowadays they call that date rape." Anger ballooned inside her, making her shake.

"You never said no. Once a slutty little tease—"

"Shut your mouth, Ted." Nate took a step forward, a muscle working in his jaw.

"My own attorney is turning on me?"

"I'm telling you not to talk to her that way."

"You believe her." Ted glared at him. "I'm your fraternity brother. What about that bond?"

"It's not a Get Out of Jail Free card."

"So you're on her side." Breathing hard, his gaze darted between her and Nate. "Thanks to you, I've got a tape to prove what I'm saying is true."

Kathryn felt as if she'd been slapped. "What are you talking about?"

"In college Nate was the Mr. Wizard of electronics. That's why we asked him to join Alpha Omega."

"So?" A cold feeling spread through her, squeezing out the rage.

"He rewired the frat house security system so we could tape in all the bedrooms."

"Oh, God—"

Nate stepped between her and Ted and grabbed him by the shirt. "I'm warning you, Ted."

The other man held out his arms, the universal innocent gesture. "Watch the threads, counselor. There must be some kind of law against roughing up your client."

Nate shook him before dropping his hands. "You're a low-life creep."

Ted's smile taunted. "Good to know some things don't change. You're still in love with Kathryn Price. At least now you don't look like you had a close encounter with a science experiment gone bad. You actually might have a shot with her." He snapped his fingers as if remembering something. "Too bad your timing is off. The way she looks now, you'd have been a better match before you got your face fixed."

"Shut up, Ted."

His blue eyes were cold with contempt. "I don't have to say a word. All I have to do is release that tape to the media. And I'll do it if you don't put more effort into my appeal and get me off the hook."

Kathryn saw Nate's hands clench into fists and when he turned, his eyes burned with fury. But when he spoke, his voice was calm. "Katie, I think you'd better leave. I need to talk to Ted and the conversation is bound by attorney-client privilege."

His fingers curled around her upper arm and were incredibly gentle considering his enraged expression. As he led her to the door, he carefully kept his body between her and Ted. Kathryn felt as if she was the star of a bad, surrealistic art film. She was just coming to terms with the fact that Nate's job involved defending bad guys. But this bad guy nearly ruined her life.

"We'll talk when I get home," he said.

Home? Where she'd felt so safe. He made the word a mockery. Everything about him was a lie.

She tugged her arm from his grasp. "I don't know who you are, Nate. And I don't want to know. You're not the man I thought. You're not even the man you led me to believe you were. I never want to see you again."

After yanking open the door, she walked out of his office and blinked hard to keep the tears from trickling down her cheeks.

When he watched Katie leave, Nate felt his anger slipping into something else and he knew he couldn't lose it. Anger, fury and rage were all he had between him and the pain he didn't want to feel. When he turned and saw the smirk on Ted's face, he could understand what drives a man to violence. If he were tried by a jury of his peers, other men who'd been hung out to dry by a fraternity brother and lost the woman they loved, he'd never be convicted for hurting Ted.

"Tough luck, bro."

Nate walked over to the other man and felt his fingers closing into fists. "First of all, don't ever call me 'bro.' Second, you don't have a tape."

"How do you know?"

"Because I disconnected the cameras when I found out what you and your slimy friends were using them for."

Ted tapped him on the chest. "But was that before or after I was with Kathryn?"

"Before." It was a bluff.

He didn't know if he'd deactivated the camera system before the night he'd comforted Kathryn—the night this bastard had assaulted her. His rage amped up again at the thought.

"Look, Nate, I'm sensing you're not on my side anymore."

"I've never been on your side, Ted. Once a weasel, always a weasel."

"So your heart wasn't in my defense." He nodded knowingly, but there was a sly, pissed-off look in his eyes. "Maybe that's why I was convicted."

"You were convicted because you're guilty of sexual assault. It's a pattern of behavior that's going to bite you in the ass. We can plead out and negotiate therapy—"

"No way." Ted's hand slashed through the air between them. "I'm innocent. She wanted it. Just like Kathryn—"

"Liar."

"I'll tell you one thing, Williams, I'm not happy with the outcome of my trial and I hold you personally responsible. I've got grounds for a legal malpractice suit."

"Go ahead. I'll countersue."

"On what grounds? I used to go out with your girlfriend?"

"Blackmail—for starters."

Ted's gaze narrowed. "Seems like I remember hearing that Kathryn was going places as a model." He tsk-tsked with insincere sympathy as he shook his head. "Now she's got to start all over, but that nasty scar kind of narrows her choices."

"What's your point, Ted?"

"I've got the tape. I'll use it. If you don't make my conviction go away, I'll see that Kathryn never works again."

Nate's rage boiled over and testosterone took control. He pulled back his arm and plowed his fist into the snarl on Ted's face, knocking him to the floor. Blood spurted and he groaned as he rolled from side to side.

"You son of a bitch, you broke my nose," he said, his voice muffled behind the hand he held over his lower face.

"Good."

Nate brushed the back of his knuckles over his mouth, then flexed his fingers. That was going to hurt later, but right now the surge of satisfaction pushed out everything else.

"Just so we're clear," he said. "You better find another firm to handle your appeal."

Ted groaned as he pushed to his feet and swayed. "You're going to regret this."

Nate shook his head. "I have a lot of regrets. But decking you won't ever be one of them."

"Watch your back, Williams." Ted left without another word.

When he was alone, Nate sat behind his desk and tried to hold on to the adrenaline rush, but it faded. Replaced by the shattered look in Katie's eyes. He'd never forget that as long as he lived.

If only he could have prepared her, brought out the facts in his own time, in his own way. He'd intended to tell her everything. Hell of a way to find out it was true that the road to hell was paved with good intentions.

Ted confirmed what Nate suspected. He'd always been in love with Katie and he knew better than to try and build anything with her on a foundation of secrets and lies. Now it would be impossible to build anything even on the truth.

Letting go of Ted's case was the easiest thing Nate had ever done; letting Katie go would bring him to his knees. But the truth was, there was nothing to let go.

He'd already lost her.

Chapter Fifteen

Kathryn was back in room 327 at the Paul Revere Inn. She'd figure out a way to scrape up the money to pay for it because she just couldn't stay with Nate. All the rhetoric in the world couldn't put a positive spin on the fact that he'd defended Ted Hawkins and never said a word to her. But her heart hurt. And it was so much worse than the trauma her body had gone through after the accident.

The meeting with Alex Broadstreet was in two days. When it was over, she would fly home to put her life back together. Odd, it felt as if her life was in more of a shambles than when she'd arrived.

There was a knock on her door and she knew the first steps to her new life were on the other side of it.

After peeking through the peephole, she opened

the door. "David. Sandra," she said. "Thank you for coming. I'm sorry I couldn't meet you in Boston."

"No problem," Sandra said. "The drive gave David and I some quiet time to talk."

David and Sandra Westport could be the poster couple for perfect. He was tall with black hair, green eyes and an athletic build that gave him the look of a sports star. And Sandra, blond, blue-eyed and cheerleader cute was his flawless match. Kathryn braced herself for their reaction to her disfigurement. They were aware of her scars, but knowing the facts and seeing her face-to-face were two different things.

"I'm glad you didn't cancel the appointment, Kathryn." Sandra took a step forward and hugged her warmly. When she stepped aside, her husband did the same.

Kathryn held out her hand toward the sofa and chairs. There was an array of beverages on the coffee table. "Won't you sit down? I've ordered coffee and tea from room service."

"Thanks." Sandra took her husband's hand as they moved to the sofa and sat side by side. He didn't let go of her fingers, until pouring her a cup of tea. The closeness between them kicked up Kathryn's envy. She could never hope for something like that. Nate was… Never mind. She wouldn't think about what could never be.

Sandra studied her intently over the rim of her cup. "I'm sorry."

"Me, too." At first Kathryn thought she meant her and Nate. Then she realized, the other woman was talking about her face.

"What happened?" David asked.

His wife shot him a glare, then sighed. "He's very blunt. It's a quality that has its good and bad points."

"Don't worry. I'll cut him some slack. Directness is something I've learned to appreciate. You should hear what Nate first said. Talk about irreverent—"

Thoughts of him brought a fresh wave of pain so powerful it stole her breath. She missed him terribly and the loss was overwhelming. So much for not thinking about him.

The other woman was still studying her. "If it's too painful to talk about—"

It took several moments for Kathryn to realize Sandra meant the accident. And she realized something else.

"I don't mind talking about it." But she would have minded. Before Nate. Now he was the painful topic she tried not to think or talk about. "I was hit almost head-on by a drunk driver."

Sandra gasped. "How awful for you."

"It's been rough," she admitted. "That's the reason I turned down your offer." She looked from husband to wife. "Which one of you came up with the camp idea?"

They looked at each other, then back at her. But it was David who spoke. "I have a lot of regrets about missed opportunities."

Kathryn could tell he was choosing his words carefully. "You're not alone. Show me a human being and I'll show you someone with regrets."

"That's what Sandy says." He glanced at his wife whose expression of respect and love never wavered.

"Anyway, I received my athletic scholarship to Saunders under suspicious circumstances. On top of that, I wasn't the best student in college. Not only did I not live up to my potential, I squandered the chance to go to school for nothing. That sort of gift needs to be repaid—and I need to make up for throwing it away. It's a moral issue, but I also want to be a positive example to my children."

"Tell me about them."

"We have twins," Sandra said. Her face took on a glow at the mention of her kids. "Michael favors me and Molly has her father's black hair and green eyes. They're ten."

Kathryn managed to hold in an envious sigh. "You're very lucky."

"Very lucky. And we try never to take it for granted." David leaned forward and rested his elbows on his knees. "A lot of kids aren't so fortunate. I could simply pay back the scholarship making it all about money. But putting that money into a sports camp for kids is something good that will last."

"It's a terrific idea," Kathryn agreed.

"We've written a proposal for a grant and the professor presented it to the benefactor who's agreed to buy the building. But that's just one hurdle. We need additional funding. Bad."

"Forgive us for taking advantage of a college acquaintance." Sandra's face took on a pleading look. "But we're hoping that you asked us to meet with you because you've changed your mind about being our celebrity spokeswoman."

"I'm not a celebrity anymore." She turned her face

toward them, letting the sunlight coming through the window draw attention to her scars and make her point. "For obvious reasons."

"We're not looking for perfection," David said. "Just commitment."

"You're recognizable," Sandra interjected. "And the fact that you've had difficulties makes your involvement even more relevant. You understand in a way no one can who hasn't been through a trauma. We need your help, Kathryn."

"I just wanted to make sure you had all the facts and still wanted me," she said. "Of course I'll do whatever I can to help you raise funds."

"Excellent." David stood and went around the table, pulling her to her feet for a bear hug. "Thank you."

Kathryn looked up at him. "No. I think I should be thanking you. I've been too self-absorbed since the accident. I'm grateful for this opportunity to channel my energy into something that's not about me."

"Speaking of your energy," David said, sitting down again. "I talked to Nate Williams."

"Oh?" Speaking of grateful, she was pleased that she managed to keep her voice normal. After hearing Nate's name, an ache settled in her chest and made breathing a challenge.

"Yeah. He pitched the idea that a certain percentage of kids accepted to the camp be recovering from facial injuries due to car accidents, or maxillofacial defects from birth."

"He mentioned the idea to me," she admitted.

"It's a great suggestion," Sandra said enthusiastically. "Not only that, he offered his legal services pro bono."

"That's Nate."

Sandra frowned. "What's wrong?"

What wasn't, Kathryn thought. Her first instinct was to clam up about her personal problems. But lately she'd realized that was a waste of energy. Ditto for trying to reconcile the sweet, sexy, supportive Nate Williams with the one who could go to bat for the bad guys. And the one who'd wired the fraternity house cameras to tape in the bedrooms.

"I just found out what kind of attorney Nate is." And what kind of man.

"A good one?" David said. "He has a reputation for being the guy you want on your side if you're in trouble."

"He represents people who have done really bad things," Kathryn protested.

"I didn't say it wasn't a dirty job." David shrugged. "But somebody has to do it."

"So I've been told." Kathryn looked from one to the other. "He represented Ted Hawkins against sexual assault charges."

"I heard about that." Disgust was evident on David's handsome face. "He was convicted."

"Rightly so, I'm sure. Ted assaulted me ten years ago."

"Oh, Kathryn." Sandra put her hand over her mouth. "I'm so sorry."

"Me, too. But that's not all. He claims he's got a tape of it from the fraternity house." She clutched her fingers together in her lap. Now that she'd agreed to their offer, Kathryn realized how much she wanted to work for the kids camp. But these good people didn't need any tabloid-worthy surprises to jeopardize their endeavor. They needed all the facts before making their final decision. "He says he's going to release it—maybe put it on the Internet. That wouldn't be the kind of publicity you want for a charity camp just getting off the ground."

"First of all," David said, "we want you no matter what. We'll stand behind you one hundred percent against Ted Hawkins. The guy is a snake and he'll probably wind up behind bars. Secondly, he's lying about having a tape."

"How do you know?"

"Nate disconnected the cameras." He leaned forward and rested his elbows on his knees, then clasped his hands. "The guys only asked him to join because he was smart and had a flair for electronics. Apparently he was IQ intelligent, but with people not so much. When he wised up, he did the right thing."

"Did you report what Ted did to you?" Sandra asked.

"No." Kathryn met her concerned gaze. "I just wanted to forget about it and I thought getting back to normal would help me do that."

"I can understand," Sandra sympathized.

"And I knew that women who suffer sexual assault often become victimized again by the legal system. I just couldn't go through that."

"Unfortunately, that's true," Sandra admitted. "But he got away with it. If you'd reported him, it would have established a record of his pattern of behavior. Who knows how many women he's assaulted? You might have prevented his latest attack. When the case made the news, David and I weren't surprised that Ted was involved."

Kathryn knew she was right. Hiding the truth only helped Ted perpetuate his violence against women. Keeping mum had only hurt her. The healing hadn't started until she'd opened up to Nate.

"So I'm the only one on the planet who didn't hear about the case?"

"You don't know what happened?" Sandra asked.

"Not a single detail. Except that Ted was convicted and the case is on appeal."

David sat back on the sofa. "Nate took a beating from legal analysts who played Monday-morning quarterback and said he should have used the victim's sexual history as part of his defense strategy."

"I didn't know," Kathryn admitted.

"We just heard on news radio that Ted hired another law firm to handle his appeal. He wants a new trial and is citing Nate's less than vigorous defense and conflict of interest." David met her gaze. "I didn't understand that part until now."

"What do you mean?"

"You're the conflict of interest. I didn't know what had happened to you, but I was at the fraternity house when Nate went after Ted—something about hurting you. Too bad in those days he was no match. Ted broke his nose."

Kathryn was stunned. Nate had never said how he'd broken his nose, just that he'd had it fixed. And that night, all he'd known was that she was crying because of Ted. Yet he'd tried to defend her, just as he'd done yesterday. Was it true that Nate had always loved her?

If not for him, she'd still be standing at a fork in the road and waiting to get flattened. Had she unfairly judged a good man? A man who was simply doing his job the best he knew how?

"Professor Harrison never liked Ted," David said. "And he was always a pretty good judge of character."

"The professor seems like a good man. I wish there wasn't so much mystery surrounding him." Sandra sighed, then looked at her husband. "It's time we headed for home."

He looked at his watch. "Yeah. We'll run into rush hour traffic if we don't head out now. We'll be in touch, Kathryn," he said, standing.

"I'll look forward to working with you both."

When they were gone, Kathryn's mind was spinning. She wondered what was really going on with the professor. Hearing David's story about repaying the scholarship reminded her of what Nate had said. Where there's smoke, there's fire. Was the professor in trouble for a reason? Scholarships and grade manipulating? Wrong thing, right reason.

And Nate. He was a good, kind, decent man. She was absolutely certain that she was in love with him. When Ted had said Nate had always loved her, she'd run scared. First of all, how could she trust Ted? Second, how could a man like Nate love the woman she was now? Worse, she'd treated him horribly. Why would he ever forgive her?

She'd burned that bridge and she would always wonder if it was the one she was meant to cross.

"Mr. Broadstreet will see you now."

Nate stood and looked at his watch, wondering for

the gazillionth time if Katie was going to show. The last thing she'd said was that she never wanted to see him again. And when he'd arrived home, she'd been gone. But this was about helping the professor.

"Mr. Williams?"

"Hmm?" He looked at the stunning secretary. Broadstreet definitely had good taste in receptionists. But could she type?

"Mr. Broadstreet is waiting."

Good. Nate wanted to ask how he liked it, but he'd probably started the clock ticking, using up their precious time to change his mind about keeping the professor on the faculty. If Katie didn't show, he'd have to go in alone.

The thought sliced into him like a chain saw through butter. He missed her more than he'd thought it was possible to miss anyone. It hadn't taken much detective work to locate her at the Paul Revere Inn, but she'd refused to take his calls. This afternoon, he'd wanted to pick her up for this meeting, but figured he'd give her some space and he could talk to her when he was through slicing and dicing Broadstreet. But if she didn't show…

Just then the outer door opened and she rushed in, starting when she saw him. "Hi."

"Hi." His heart hammered and relief flooded him like coastal lowlands during a tropical storm.

"Sorry I'm late. I—"

"Doesn't matter," he said sincerely. As long as she was there, he didn't care. "Let's go see Mr. Broadstreet."

She nodded and he stood by the door to the inner

sanctum, opening it when she approached. The sweet, familiar fragrance of her perfume filled him with longing. But he put it aside and followed her into the office.

Alexander Broadstreet sat behind his desk like a Supreme Court Justice who held sway over the fate of a country. He was in his early forties, his attitude one of cool sophistication. If the vacant look in his pale blue eyes was any gauge, he was also a heartless bastard. And his single-minded crusade to replace the professor proved you could judge a book by its cover.

"Miss Price," he said after Katie introduced herself.

"How do you do, Mr. Broadstreet?"

He studied her as he shook the hand she held out. "The same Kathryn Price who was once the face of that major cosmetics company?"

"Yes."

Nate shot her a quick glance and saw that she'd taken the question in stride. She'd come a long way from the woman he'd seen hiding behind her sunglasses.

"My wife, Alicia, is quite fond of those products. Although she's a naturally beautiful woman, who needs no cosmetics," he added insincerely.

"That's nice of you to say and I'm sure she appreciates your regard."

"I don't believe I've seen your work recently."

Katie's chin lifted as she met his gaze. "I've been out of the business for a little over a year. An accident."

"I'm sorry to hear that." He looked away. "And you're Nate Williams."

Nate studied the man's practiced smile and won-

dered if it worked to charm money and favors from un-
suspecting marks. His blond hair was perfectly
trimmed and combed, not a strand out of place. There
was nothing out of place in his office, either. Expensive mahogany bookcases were a backdrop to the
matching desk. That and the high-backed black leather
chair behind it had most likely set the university back
a buck or two. Guys like Broadstreet expected someone else to pay for the trimmings.

He held out his hand. "Broadstreet."

"You look very familiar." The other man's grip was
soft as he stared. "You're *the* Nate Williams, gifted defense attorney?"

"Guilty," Nate said.

"I followed the Ted Hawkins case. He's an alumni,
after all. And a generous contributor to the college.
Pity about his conviction."

If the gleam in the other man's eyes was any indica-
tion, Broadstreet's interest was aroused and he was
looking for another score. "This is a pleasure, Nate.
May I call you that?"

"Of course, Alex."

"Had I realized who you are, I'd have made room
in my busy schedule sooner."

If anyone had told Nate he'd have something to
thank Alex Broadstreet for, he'd have thought they
were crazy. He'd lost Katie, and that was his own fault.
But thanks to Broadstreet keeping them waiting for
this appointment, Nate had been able to spend time
with her. He'd made memories to cherish and sustain
him for the rest of his life.

"Please sit down," he said, indicating the two

leather wing chairs in front of his desk. "Both of you," he said, barely glancing at Katie. The snub was obvious. She was useless to Broadstreet because she was off the publicity radar.

Nate held on to his temper. Losing it now would be counterproductive. "Thank you," he said, waiting for her to sit first, then taking a seat.

"So what brings you here today, Nate?"

"Katie and I are here to see you about Professor Harrison," he began. "To put in a good word for a former teacher who made a difference in both our lives."

"That's right," Katie chimed in.

"The professor personally nurtured me at a time when I had no one to turn to."

Broadstreet didn't need to know about altering grades. After the fact Nate had suspected the truth, but he'd chosen not to question his luck. He regretted that and would always wonder if it hadn't contributed to the less than positive path he'd chosen. He couldn't change the past; he could only try to do better now. And use the techniques he'd honed as a trial lawyer on the professor's behalf.

"If not for Gilbert Harrison, there's no question in my mind that I wouldn't be where I am today."

Broadstreet nodded. "One of the most famous, sought-after and high-priced attorneys in the country. Also a Saunders alumni."

"Who learned from Saunders' finest. Professor Harrison has a sharp mind and a way of bringing out the best in young people. He's an asset to any faculty. This university is lucky to have him on staff."

Katie took a deep breath. "The professor was the

first one to challenge me to be more. He encouraged me to be a good student and not simply rely on surface talents."

"And a good thing, too," Alex said, his cinema smile slipping into pity as he looked at her scarred face.

Katie didn't flinch. "I couldn't agree more. The professor is a firm believer in hoping for the best but preparing for the worst. Have a backup plan."

"Indeed."

"Yes. And I'm appalled that you, and the board of directors of Saunders University are trying to get rid of him. He had a lot to offer when I was a student here. And he has a lot to offer future students. In fact, when I first arrived several weeks ago, he shared words of wisdom that helped me through a personal crisis."

Nate could see by the bored expression on Broadstreet's face that their character testimonials were a waste of breath. And revealing the professor's greatest gift would be like putting a felon on the witness stand and opening the door for a prosecution cross-examination that would get on record every bad thing he'd ever done.

"My dear," he said, in a voice rife with condescension. "Sentiment is all well and good. But it doesn't pay the bills, if you know what I mean."

Nate frowned. "Why do I have a feeling the almighty dollar is at the heart of your campaign to get rid of the professor?"

The charming facade slipped momentarily, then it was back in place. "Nate, you of all people should know that there's a price tag on time. The board and faculty here at Saunders have agreed on an image and a plan for the university. We intend to court athletes and young people who will go on to careers in which they'll be in a position to give back to their alma mater. Every time you handle a high-profile case your personal information is in the media. It occurs to me that you could be a great asset in fund-raising."

"Is it the university you're interested in?" he asked. "Or simply surrounding yourself with the wealthy and famous and positioning yourself in the public eye?"

The other man abandoned the smile. "The university is always uppermost in my mind. But when an athlete is touted on Monday night football, inevitably his background is mentioned from coast to coast—including the institution of higher education that he attended. That translates into revenue."

Nate stood and moved closer to the desk, putting his palms flat on the top as he leaned forward. "So are you saying when it comes to Saunders applications for enrollment, geeks need not apply?"

"Of course not." He rested his elbows on his desk and steepled his fingers. "All applications will be scrutinized and Saunders University will accept the cream of the crop."

"Athletically," Nate challenged.

"It's a plus," the other man admitted.

Nate straightened and stared down at him. "By those standards, I'd have a different university on my résumé."

The other man studied him, clearly puzzled. "Oh?"

"Yeah. I was head geek in my days here at Saunders."

"I find that hard to believe."

Katie stood. "It's reprehensible that you've made it your mission to get rid of a gifted teacher because he doesn't happen to share your vision of the future."

"And if that teacher has thumbed his nose at the regulations and policies?" Broadstreet stood and assumed an arrogant, intimidating pose. "An educator who ignores the rules isn't fit to be a role model here at Saunders."

"Administrators on a vendetta or using a position of authority for personal gain have no place in the educational process, either," Nate said.

"There will be a formal hearing to uncover all the facts," he said coldly. "Now, if you'll both excuse me, I'm very busy."

Nate looked at Katie. "I guess we're done here."

She nodded and he opened the door for her, then looked back at the man who held the professor's fate in his hands. "Just in case you didn't get it, your plan to undermine the professor's support among his former students didn't work. I'll be back for that formal hearing along with more of the professor's former students."

Nate was so proud of her. The feeling was bittersweet because he'd never loved her more. And she'd never been further out of his reach. But he forced a grin. "I couldn't have said it better myself."

Broadstreet frowned. "Is that a threat, counselor?"

"No. A promise."

If only his life had promise, Nate thought. He closed the door behind him and looked down at Katie. This was the last time he would see her.

Chapter Sixteen

Kathryn had rarely been so enraged in her life. When Alex Broadstreet had dismissed her because she was scarred and of no use to him, then went after Nate who was wealthy and well-known, she'd wanted to choke the college administrator with her bare hands. The underhanded weasel had unleashed the paparazzi on her because he thought she was a famous model. He hadn't known her secret. But she was free of them all now. Except one—her love for the man beside her.

After walking out of the Administration building they kept going and as if by mutual consent, stopped by the fountain where he'd comforted her that night long ago.

"That man is vermin. He's a vulture." Kathryn hesitated, so angry she could hardly think straight. "If I were as good with words as you, I'd be able to think of another *V* name to call him."

"Voracious, as in money and power."

"Good word." A warm breeze blew her hair across her face and she tucked it behind her ear. "Did you see the way he dismissed me when he got it that my career isn't what it used to be?"

"Yeah. I noticed."

She blew out a long breath. "That was a colossal waste of time. I just hope when the board meets to decide what's happening with Professor Gilbert, all of his former students together can make them listen to reason and save his job. There's still so much good work he can do. Alex Broadstreet is a single-minded, cold-hearted, social-climbing creep."

"Yeah."

"He reminds me of Ted," she said quietly, meeting Nate's gaze.

His eyes filled with regret and pain as he slid his fingers into the pockets of his slacks. In his perfectly fitted navy pinstriped suit and red power tie, he looked every bit the wealthy, well-known attorney. But she knew he was so much more. Since she had a plane to catch in a couple of hours, this would probably be her only opportunity to tell him.

"Nate, I—"

"Katie, let me—" They both spoke at the same time.

"You first," she said.

He didn't hesitate. "As you've pointed out I'm a

lawyer and words are my life. I pride myself on finding the right ones, but I don't have them now to tell you how sorry I am."

"You don't have to—"

"Yes. I do. Let me explain. When Ted was arrested, he called me because of my reputation and the fact that we were fraternity brothers and are supposed to have a bond. You know better than anyone how I felt about him. Couldn't stomach the son of a bitch. I was going to refuse the case."

"Why didn't you?" She didn't ask because she needed to know. She asked because he needed to tell her.

"It went to a show of hands at the firm. The partners outvoted me and I had to take it on."

"I see."

"Ironically, Ted accused me of incompetence. The complaint may actually have merit if he decides to pursue a malpractice suit against me. I don't think the defense I mounted was as vigorous as it could have been."

"Because you wouldn't bring up the victim's sexual history and victimize her again?"

"Yes, but—" He stared at her. "How did you know that? I thought you didn't watch the news."

"The Westports told me. By the way, David said Ted was bluffing. There's no tape. Because you disconnected the cameras when you found out what they were being used for."

"I couldn't remember if that was before or after the night he—hurt you." But he let out a sigh of relief. "It's good to know, even though there's not a chance in hell he'd use one if he had it. I'd bury him and he knows it."

"They said he hired another firm to handle the appeal, citing conflict of interest." She held her hand to her forehead, shielding her eyes from the sun as she met his gaze. "What conflict would that be?"

Did it have anything to do with the fact that he loved her and couldn't be objective?

Nate hesitated, as if picking his words carefully. "It's about the past," he finally said.

Kathryn wanted him to say more. She wanted it to be about her, about the fact that he cared. This time she wanted to hear it from Nate. And she would because he'd taught her not to let anything stop her.

He ran his fingers through his hair and she noticed his scraped knuckles. She reached out and took his hand in hers, studying the scabbed-over marks. "What happened?"

"A close encounter with Ted's nose." He grinned, a look filled with supreme male satisfaction. "That's part of the reason he went to another firm. Decking your client could be defined a conflict of interest."

"So it went better this time?"

"What?" he asked, confused.

"Punching Ted. The Westports also told me how you went after him—that night, on my behalf. When you thought I was upset because we'd broken up."

"Yeah." He shrugged. "The spirit was willing and I had testosterone to spare. But I hadn't taken self-defense 101."

"He broke your nose."

"I returned the favor."

"And?"

"And I can give him the name of a gifted plastic surgeon here in Boston."

His grin made her legs weak even as her heart hammered. "I—I can give him the name of one in L.A."

Nate laughed. "He's going to need more than a doctor when the legal system gets through with him. He can appeal from now to kingdom come but the DNA evidence and police photos along with the victim's testimony will sink him. I just wish she didn't have to go through that."

"She went straight to the authorities?" Kathryn caught her top lip between her teeth. When he nodded, she said, "I wish I had. It might have prevented him hurting her and God knows how many other women."

"You had your reasons, Katie," he said gently.

"They weren't good enough. I'll always be sorry I didn't do something to stop him then. But I'm not sorry you got even with Ted for what he did to you. One of many secrets I know about you now."

His expression was rueful. "I planned to tell you everything—the night Rachel stopped by. If I had—"

She shook her head. "The point is I know now. I also know you're donating your legal expertise pro bono to Sandra and David for the sports camp."

One of his eyebrows arched. "That was quite a meeting you had with the Westports."

"Yes, it was. I've agreed to be the public face for their charity."

"That's great." He grinned and started to pull her into a hug, but stopped and let his hands drop to his sides.

"They don't know it yet, but I'm going to be the first contributor."

"Oh?"

"I've contacted a reporter for *Star Secrets*—"

"The tabloid rag?" he asked, obviously surprised.

She nodded. "They pay the best."

"What are you selling them?"

"The first photograph of Kathryn Price's face, post-accident."

"Katie—" He looked doubtful. "Are you sure you want to do that?"

She nodded. "The difference is I'm doing it on my terms. The resulting publicity for the sports camp is something money can't buy. And I plan to donate my fee to the Westport Kids' Camp."

His look of admiration warmed her. "You're amazing. They're lucky to have you."

"I hope so. I'm lucky to have them."

"I guess this means you found yourself?"

She nodded. "The professor was right. It took coming back to my roots to figure out who I am."

His expression turned serious. "You're not the only one who was lost. I didn't like the face I saw in the mirror while I was here at Saunders. But as an attorney, I hated the face even more—and not because of scars. Money is important, but you can't put a price tag on honor. And I won't compromise mine any longer."

"I don't think you're capable of compromising honor. You're the most admirable man I've ever met."

He shook his head. "I haven't been, but I plan to change that. Everyone is entitled to a vigorous defense. But I plan to pick and choose my cases more carefully and take the ones I believe in. The circling sharks who smell the blood in the water can have the rest."

"Nate, you don't have to do this on my account—"

He stopped her with a finger to her lips. "It's on my account. Everything isn't black and white, but I can't live in the gray area anymore. I need to put color back into my world." He cupped her face in his palm and traced the scar on her cheek with his thumb. Then he dropped his hand. "I can't remember a time when I didn't love you. But I understand why you can't feel the same about me."

She shook her head and sighed. "The smarter they are..."

"What?"

"I have regrets, too. The biggest one is what I said to you that day in your office. I was wrong and I'm hoping you can forgive me." She met his gaze and willed him to understand. "I've lived through an assault, earthquakes and a car accident. I've learned that if I take life one day at a time, eventually the pain recedes. But not seeing you this last couple of days..." She stared into the distance, struggling to find the words. "I know in my heart that living day after day without you will multiply my pain a hundredfold. And that's no life at all."

He searched her gaze. "Katie?"

"I always knew you were a good man. There's nothing gray about that. Seeing Ted was a shock, I'll admit.

But the truth is I was looking for an excuse to push you away."

"Why?" he asked, clearly puzzled.

"Because I was afraid you couldn't love me. Not the way I look."

He pulled her into his arms. "And I thought if you knew my secrets, you couldn't love me, that my flaws were too much."

She rubbed the left side of her face against his chest. "No one knows better than me that everyone has flaws, inside and out. It's those very imperfections that give us our humanity."

He held her away from him and stared into her eyes, a spark of hope lighting his own. "I couldn't agree more."

"You are the most decent, loving man I've ever known. When I saw you again, it was as if my heart remembered your heart. Even though I didn't recognize you on the outside, I was drawn to the kindness and innate honesty I remembered and I instantly trusted you even though I hadn't been able to trust for a very long time. You helped me find strength I didn't know I had. You are—"

He touched a finger to her mouth. "Words are highly overrated. Could you please cut to the chase? You're killing me here."

"You are the man I love with all my heart."

"Thank God." He let out a long breath and the intensity in his eyes spoke volumes. "Stay with me, Katie. I don't know if I have the right to ask, but I can't help it. Before you answer, you have to know this. Whether you go or stay, I'll love you every day for the rest of my life the way I do right now. I love you with all my heart. It started in college, and I never got over you. So stay. Please?"

"Just try and get rid of me. For good measure, if you don't ask me to marry you, you're going to force me to do it. Since I'm an old-fashioned girl at heart…"

"With pleasure." He dropped to one knee. "Kathryn Price—"

"Katie," she corrected.

He smiled and nodded with satisfaction. "Katie, will you marry me?"

"Yes." She said it without hesitation. Why should there be when she'd been waiting for him ten long years?

He stood and pulled her into his arms and she linked her hands around his neck as he lowered his mouth to hers. He lifted her off her feet and kissed her until she felt all the love he'd carried around inside him flow into her. She knew he would always take care of her as he'd done all those years ago and was doing even now. And she would take care of him right back.

When he set her gently on her feet, he said, "I want to tell everyone that the most beautiful girl in the world has agreed to marry me."

"Can we tell the professor first?"

"I think that would be fitting," he agreed. "After all, we have more than the past to thank him for. We have a future."

"Yes, we do. And it includes coming here together,

and presenting a united front on his behalf when his future is on the line."

"It's a deal and I think we should seal it symbolically. Kiss me, Katie."

"With pleasure."

And for a very long time, they sealed the deal and the promises made to spend the rest of their lives loving each other.

* * * * *

Look for THE MEASURE OF A MAN
by bestselling author Marie Ferrarella,
the next book in the new Special Edition continuity,
MOST LIKELY TO…
And find out what surprises are in store
for Professor Harrison's
single-mom secretary when she falls for the man
helping her investigate her boss!
On sale September 2005
only from Silhouette Books.

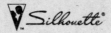

If you enjoyed what you just read,
then we've got an offer you can't resist!

Take 2 bestselling love stories FREE!

Plus get a FREE surprise gift!

COMING NEXT MONTH

SPECIAL EDITION

#1705 HOME AGAIN—Joan Elliott Pickart
After a miscarriage left her unable to bear children and her high school sweetheart divorced her, child psychologist Cedar Kennedy vowed never to love again. But when humble construction company owner Mark Chandler brought his orphaned nephew, Joey, in for treatment, Cedar sensed she'd met a man who could rebuild her capacity for love....

#1706 THE MEASURE OF A MAN—Marie Ferrarella
Most Likely To...
Divorced mom Jane Jackson took a job at her alma mater to pay the bills...and now used it to access confidential records seeking information about the anonymous benefactor who'd paid for her education. For help getting to the files, she turned to the school's maintenance man, Smith Parker. Did this sensitive but emotionally scarred man hold the key to her past—and her future?

#1707 THE TYCOON'S MARRIAGE BID—
Allison Leigh
When six-months-pregnant Nikki Day collapsed on her vacation, she awoke with former boss Alexander Reed by her bedside. Alex devoted himself to Nikki's care, even in the face of his estranged father's attempts to take over his business. Their feelings for each other grew—but she was carrying his cousin's baby. And Alex had a secret, too....

#1708 THE OTHER SIDE OF PARADISE—Laurie Paige
Seven Devils
The minute Mary McHale arrived for her wrangler job at a ranch in the Seven Devils Mountains, her boss, Jonah Lanigan, had eyes for her. Then Mary, orphaned at an early age, noticed her own striking resemblance to the Daltons on the neighboring ranch. After discovering her true identity—and true love with Jonah—would she have to choose between the two?

#1709 TAMING A DARK HORSE—Stella Bagwell
Men of the West
After suffering serious burns rescuing his horses from a fire, loner Linc Ketchum needed Nevada Ortiz's help. The sassy home nurse brought Linc back to health and kindled a flame in his heart. But ever since his mother had abandoned him as a child, Linc just couldn't trust a woman. Now Nevada needed to find a cure...for Linc's wounded spirit.

#1710 UNDERCOVER NANNY—Wendy Warren
As nanny to restaurateur Maxwell Lotorto's four foster kids, sultry Daisy June "D.J." Holden had ulterior motives—she was really a private eye, hired to find out if her boss was the missing heir to a supermarket dynasty. D.J. fell hard for Max's charms—not to mention the unruly kids. But would her secret bring their newfound happiness to an abrupt end?